After Dark

Haruki Murakami

After Dark

TRANSLATED

FROM THE

JAPANESE

BY JAY RUBIN

ALFRED A. KNOPF

NEW YORK · 2007

THIS IS A BORZOI BOOK
PUBLISHED BY
ALFRED A. KNOPF

Translation copyright © 2007
by Haruki Murakami

All rights reserved. Published in the United
States by Alfred A. Knopf, a division of
Random House, Inc., New York.

www.aaknopf.com

Originally published in Japan as Afutādāku
by Kodansha, Tokyo, in 2004. Copyright
© 2004 by Haruki Murakami

Knopf, Borzoi Books, and the colophon
are registered trademarks of Random
House, Inc.

Library of Congress Cataloging-in-
Publication Data

Murakami, Haruki, [date]
[Afutadaku. English]
After dark / by Haruki Murakami ;
translated from the Japanese by Jay Rubin.
p. cm.
ISBN-13: 978-0-307-26583-8
I. Rubin, Jay   II. Title.
PL856.U673A6613 2007
895.6'35—dc22   2007004828

Manufactured in the United States
of America

FIRST UNITED STATES EDITION

After Dark

O p.m.

1

Eyes mark the shape of the city.

Through the eyes of a high-flying night bird, we take in the scene from midair. In our broad sweep, the city looks like a single gigantic creature—or more like a single collective entity created by many intertwining organisms. Countless arteries stretch to the ends of its elusive body, circulating a continuous supply of fresh blood cells, sending out new data and collecting the old, sending out new consumables and collecting the old, sending out new contradictions and collecting the old. To the rhythm of its pulsing, all parts of the body flicker and flare up and squirm. Midnight is approaching, and while the peak of activity has passed, the basal metabolism that maintains life continues undiminished, producing the basso continuo of the city's moan, a monotonous sound that neither rises nor falls but is pregnant with foreboding.

Our line of sight chooses an area of concentrated brightness and, focusing there, silently descends to it—a sea of neon colors. They call this place an "amusement district." The giant digital screens fastened to the sides of buildings fall silent as midnight approaches, but loudspeakers on storefronts keep pumping out exaggerated hip-hop bass lines. A large game center crammed with young people; wild electronic sounds; a group of college students spilling out from a bar; teenage girls with brilliant bleached hair, healthy legs thrusting out from micromini skirts; dark-suited men racing across diagonal crosswalks for the last trains to the suburbs. Even at this hour, the karaoke club pitchmen keep shouting for customers. A flashy black station wagon drifts down the street as if taking stock of the district through its black-tinted windows. The car looks like a deep-sea creature with specialized skin and organs. Two young policemen patrol the street with tense expressions, but no one seems to notice them. The district plays by its own rules at a time like this. The season is late autumn. No wind is blowing, but the air carries a chill. The date is just about to change.

We are inside a Denny's.

Unremarkable but adequate lighting; expressionless decor and dinnerware; floor plan designed to the last detail by management engineers; innocuous background music at low volume; staff meticulously trained to deal with customers by the book: "Welcome to Denny's." Everything about the restaurant is anonymous and interchangeable. And almost every seat is filled.

After a quick survey of the interior, our eyes come to rest on a girl sitting by the front window. Why her? Why not someone else? Hard to say. But, for some reason, she attracts our attention—very naturally. She sits at a four-person table, reading a book. Hooded gray parka, blue jeans, yellow sneakers faded from repeated washing. On the back of the chair next to her hangs a varsity jacket. This, too, is far from new. She is probably college freshman age, though an air of high school still clings to her. Hair black, short, and straight. Little makeup, no jewelry. Small, slender face. Black-rimmed glasses. Every now and then, an earnest wrinkle forms between her brows.

She reads with great concentration. Her eyes rarely move from the pages of her book—a thick hardback. A bookstore wrapper hides the title from us. Judging from her intent expression, the book might contain challenging subject matter. Far from skimming, she seems to be biting off and chewing it one line at a time.

On her table is a coffee cup. And an ashtray. Next to the ashtray, a navy blue baseball cap with a Boston Red Sox "B." It might be a little too large for her head. A brown leather shoulder bag rests on the seat next to her. It bulges as if its contents had been thrown in on the spur of the moment. She reaches out at regular intervals and brings the coffee cup to her mouth, but she doesn't appear to be enjoying the flavor. She drinks because she has a cup of coffee in front of her: that is her role as a customer. At odd moments, she puts a cigarette between her lips and lights it with a plastic lighter. She narrows her eyes, releases an easy puff of smoke into the air, puts the cigarette into the ashtray, and then, as if to soothe an approaching headache, she strokes her temples with her fingertips.

The music playing at low volume is "Go Away Little Girl" by Percy Faith and His Orchestra. No one is listening, of course. Many different kinds of people are taking meals and drinking coffee in this late-night Denny's, but

5

she is the only female there alone. She raises her face from her book now and then to glance at her watch, but she seems dissatisfied with the slow passage of time. Not that she appears to be waiting for anyone: she doesn't look around the restaurant or train her eyes on the front door. She just keeps reading her book, lighting an occasional cigarette, mechanically tipping back her coffee cup, and hoping for the time to pass a little faster. Needless to say, dawn will not be here for hours.

She breaks off her reading and looks outside. From this second-story window she can look down on the busy street. Even at a time like this, the street is bright enough and filled with people coming and going—people with places to go and people with no place to go; people with a purpose and people with no purpose; people trying to hold time back and people trying to urge it forward. After a long, steady look at this jumbled street scene, she holds her breath for a moment and turns her eyes once again toward her book. She reaches for her coffee cup. Puffed no more than two or three times, her cigarette turns into a perfectly formed column of ash in the ashtray.

The electric door slides open and a lanky young man walks in. Short black leather coat, wrinkled olive-green chinos, brown work boots. Hair fairly long and tangled in places. Perhaps he has had no chance to wash it in some days. Perhaps he has just crawled out of the underbrush somewhere. Or perhaps he just finds it more natural and comfortable to have messy hair. His thinness makes him look less elegant than malnourished. A big black instrument case hangs from his shoulder. Wind instrument. He also holds a dirty tote bag at his side. It seems to be stuffed with sheet music and other assorted things. His right cheek bears an eye-catching scar. It is short and deep, as if the flesh has been gouged out by something sharp. Nothing else about him stands out. He is a very ordinary young man with the air of a nice—but not very clever—stray mutt.

The waitress on hostess duty shows him to a seat at the back of the restaurant. He passes the table of the girl with the book. A few steps beyond it, he comes to a halt as if a thought has struck him. He begins moving slowly backward as in a rewinding film, stopping at her table. He cocks his head and studies her face. He is trying to remember something, and much time goes by until he gets it. He seems like the type for whom everything takes time.

The girl senses his presence and raises her face from her book. She narrows her eyes and looks at the young man standing there. He is so tall, she seems to be looking far overhead. Their eyes meet. The young man smiles. His smile is meant to show he means no harm.

Sorry if I've got the wrong person," he says, "but aren't you Eri Asai's little sister?"

She does not answer. She looks at him with eyes that could be looking at an overgrown bush in the corner of a garden.

"We met once," he continues. "Your name is . . . Yuri . . . sort of like your sister Eri's except the first syllable."

Keeping a cautious gaze fixed on him, she executes a concise factual correction: "Mari."

7

He raises his index finger and says, "That's it! Mari. Eri and Mari. Different first syllables. You don't remember me, do you?"

Mari inclines her head slightly. This could mean either yes or no. She takes off her glasses and sets them down beside her coffee cup.

The waitress retraces her steps and asks, "Are you together?"

"Uh-huh," he answers. "We are."

She sets his menu on the table. He takes the seat across from Mari and puts his case on the seat next to his. A moment later he thinks to ask Mari, "Mind if I sit here a while? I'll get out as soon as I'm finished eating. I have to meet somebody."

Mari gives him a slight frown. "Aren't you supposed to say that *before* you sit down?"

He thinks about the meaning of her words. "That I have to meet somebody?"

"No . . . ," Mari says.

"Oh, you mean as a matter of politeness."

"Uh-huh."

He nods. "You're right. I should have asked if it's okay to sit at your table. I'm sorry. But the place is crowded, and I won't bother you for long. Do you mind?"

Mari gives her shoulders a little shrug that seems to mean "As you wish." He opens his menu and studies it.

"Are you through eating?" he asks.

"I'm not hungry."

With a scowl, he scans the menu, snaps it shut, and lays it on the table. "I really don't have to open the menu," he says. "I'm just faking it."

8

Mari doesn't say anything.

"I don't eat anything but chicken salad here. Ever. If you ask me, the only thing worth eating at Denny's is the chicken salad. I've had just about everything on the menu. Have you ever tried their chicken salad?"

Mari shakes her head.

"It's not bad. Chicken salad and crispy toast. That's all I ever eat at Denny's."

"So why do you even bother looking at the menu?"

He pulls at the wrinkles in the corner of one eye with his pinky finger. "Just think about it. Wouldn't it be too sad to walk into Denny's and order chicken salad without looking at the menu? It's like telling the world, 'I come to Denny's all the time because I love the chicken salad.' So I always go through the motion of opening the menu and pretending I picked the chicken salad after considering other things."

The waitress brings him water and he orders chicken salad and crispy toast. "Make it really crispy," he says with conviction. "Almost burnt." He also orders coffee for afterwards. The waitress inputs his order using a hand-held device and confirms it by reading it aloud.

"And I think the young lady needs a refill," he says, pointing at Mari's cup.

"Thank you, sir. I will bring the coffee right away."

He watches her go off.

"You don't like chicken?" he asks.

"It's not that," Mari says. "But I make a point of not eating chicken out."

"Why not?"

"Especially the chicken they serve in chain restaurants—

9

they're full of weird drugs. Growth hormones and stuff. The chickens are locked in these dark, narrow cages, and given all these shots, and their feed is full of chemicals, and they're put on conveyor belts, and machines cut their heads off and pluck them . . ."

"Whoa!" he says with a smile. The wrinkles at the corners of his eyes deepen. "Chicken salad à la George Orwell!"

Mari narrows her eyes and looks at him. She can't tell if he is making fun of her.

"Anyhow," he says, "the chicken salad here is not bad. Really."

As if suddenly recalling that he is wearing it, he takes off his leather coat, folds it, and lays it on the seat next to his. Then he rubs his hands together atop the table. He has on a green, coarse-knit crew-neck sweater. Like his hair, the wool of the sweater is tangled in places. He is obviously not the sort who pays a lot of attention to his appearance.

"We met at a hotel swimming pool in Shinagawa. Two summers ago. Remember?"

"Sort of."

"My buddy was there, your sister was there, you were there, and I was there. Four of us all together. We had just entered college, and I'm pretty sure you were in your second year of high school. Right?"

Mari nods without much apparent interest.

"My friend was kinda dating your sister then. He brought me along on like a double date. He dug up four free tickets to the pool, and your sister brought you along. You hardly said a word, though. You spent the whole time in the pool, swimming like a young dolphin. We went to the hotel tea room for ice cream afterwards. You ordered a peach melba."

Mari frowns. "How come you remember stuff like that?"

"I never dated a girl who ate peach melba before. And you were cute, of course."

Mari looks at him blankly. "Liar. You were staring at my sister the whole time."

"I was?"

Mari answers with silence.

"Maybe I was," he says. "For some reason I remember her bikini was really tiny."

Mari pulls out a cigarette, puts it between her lips, and lights it with her lighter.

"Let me tell you something," he says. "I'm not trying to defend Denny's or anything, but I'm pretty sure that smoking a whole pack of cigarettes is *way* worse for you than eating a plate of chicken salad that *might* have some problems with it. Don't you think so?"

Mari ignores his question.

"Another girl was supposed to go with my sister that time, but she got sick at the last minute and my sister forced me to go with her. To keep the numbers right."

"So you were in a bad mood."

"I remember you, though."

"Really?"

Mari puts her finger on her right cheek.

The young man touches the deep scar on his own cheek. "Oh, this. When I was a kid, I was going too fast on my bike and couldn't make the turn at the bottom of the hill. Another inch and I would have lost my right eye. My earlobe's deformed, too. Wanna see it?"

Mari frowns and shakes her head.

The waitress brings the chicken salad and toast to the table. She pours fresh coffee into Mari's cup and checks to make sure she has brought all the ordered items to the table. He picks up his knife and fork and, with practiced movements, begins eating his chicken salad. Then he picks up a piece of toast, stares at it, and wrinkles his brow.

"No matter how much I scream at them to make my toast as crispy as possible, I have never once gotten it the way I want it. I can't imagine why. What with Japanese industriousness and high-tech culture and the market principles that the Denny's chain is always pursuing, it shouldn't be that hard to get crispy toast, don't you think? So, why can't they do it? Of what value is a civilization that can't toast a piece of bread as ordered?"

Mari doesn't take him up on this.

"But anyhow, your sister was a real beauty," the young man says, as if talking to himself.

Mari looks up. "Why do you say that in the past tense?"

"Why do I . . . ? I mean, I'm talking about something that happened a long time ago, so I used the past tense, that's all. I'm not saying she isn't a beauty now or anything."

"She's still pretty, I think."

"Well, that's just dandy. But, to tell you the truth, I don't know Eri Asai all that well. We were in the same class for a year in high school, but I hardly said two words to her. It might be more accurate to say she wouldn't give me the time of day."

"You're still interested in her, right?"

The young man stops his knife and fork in midair and thinks for a moment. "Interested. Hmm. Maybe as a kind of intellectual curiosity."

"Intellectual curiosity?"

"Yeah, like, what would it feel like to go out on a date with a beautiful girl like Eri Asai? I mean, she's an absolute cover girl."

"You call that *intellectual* curiosity?"

"Kind of, yeah."

"But back then, your friend was the one going out with her, and you were the other guy on a double date."

He nods with a mouthful of food, which he then takes all the time he needs to chew.

"I'm kind of a low-key guy. The spotlight doesn't suit me. I'm more of a side dish—cole slaw or French fries or a Wham! backup singer."

"Which is why you were paired with me."

"But still, you were pretty damn cute."

"Is there something about your personality that makes you prefer the past tense?"

The young man smiles. "No, I was just directly expressing how I felt back then from the perspective of the present. You were very cute. Really. You hardly talked to me, though."

He rests his knife and fork on his plate, takes a drink of water, and wipes his mouth with a paper napkin. "So, while you were swimming, I asked Eri Asai, 'Why won't your little sister talk to me? Is there something wrong with me?' "

"What'd she say?"

"That you never take the initiative to talk to anybody. That you're kinda different, and that even though you're Japanese you speak more often in Chinese than Japanese. So I shouldn't worry. She didn't think there was anything especially wrong with me."

Mari silently crushes her cigarette out in the ashtray.

"It's true, isn't it? There wasn't anything especially wrong with me, was there?"

Mari thinks for a moment. "I don't remember all that well, but I don't think there was anything wrong with you."

"That's good. I was worried. Of course, I *do* have a few things wrong with me, but those are strictly problems I keep inside. I'd hate to think they were obvious to anybody else. Especially at a swimming pool in the summer."

Mari looks at him again as if to confirm the accuracy of his statement. "I don't think I was aware of any problems you had inside."

"That's a relief."

"I can't remember your name, though," Mari says.

"My name?"

"Your name."

He shakes his head. "I don't mind if you forgot my name. It's about as ordinary as a name can be. Even I feel like forgetting it sometimes. It's not that easy, though, to forget your own name. Other people's names—even ones I have to remember—I'm always forgetting."

He glances out the window as if in search of something he should not have lost. Then he turns toward Mari again.

"One thing always mystified me, and that is, why didn't your sister ever get into the pool that time? It was a hot day, and a really nice pool."

Mari looks at him as if to say, *You mean you don't get that, either?* "She didn't want her makeup to wash off. It's so obvious. And you can't really swim in a bathing suit like that."

"Is that it?" he says. "It's amazing how two sisters can be so different."

"We live two different lives."

He thinks about her words for a few moments and then says, "I wonder how it turns out that we all lead such different lives. Take you and your sister, for example. You're born to the same parents, you grow up in the same household, you're both girls. How do you end up with such wildly different personalities? At what point do you, like, go your separate ways? One puts on a bikini like little semaphore flags and lies by the pool looking sexy, and the other puts on her school bathing suit and swims her heart out like a dolphin . . ."

Mari looks at him. "Are you asking me to explain it to you here and now in twenty-five words or less while you eat your chicken salad?"

He shakes his head. "No, I was just saying what popped into my head out of curiosity or something. You don't have to answer. I was just asking myself."

He starts to work on his chicken salad again, changes his mind, and continues:

"I don't have any brothers or sisters, so I just wanted to know: up to what point do they resemble each other, and where do their differences come in?"

Mari remains silent while the young man with the knife and fork in his hands stares thoughtfully at a point in space above the table.

Then he says, "I once read a story about three brothers who washed up on an island in Hawaii. A myth. An old one. I read it when I was a kid, so I probably don't have the story exactly right, but it goes something like this. Three brothers went out fishing and got caught in a storm. They drifted on the ocean for a long time until they washed up on the shore of an uninhabited island. It was a beautiful island with coconuts growing there and tons of fruit on the trees, and a big, high mountain in the middle. The night they got there, a god appeared in their dreams and said, 'A little farther down the shore, you will find three big, round boulders. I want each of you to push his boulder as far as he likes. The place you stop pushing your boulder is where you will live. The higher you go, the more of the world you will be able to see from your home. It's entirely up to you how far you want to push your boulder.'"

The young man takes a drink of water and pauses for a moment. Mari looks bored, but she is clearly listening.

"Okay so far?" he asks.

Mari nods.

"Want to hear the rest? If you're not interested, I can stop."

"If it's not too long."

"No, it's not too long. It's a pretty simple story."

He takes another sip of water and continues with his story.

"So the three brothers found three boulders on the shore just as the god had said they would. And they started pushing them along as the god told them to. Now these were huge, heavy boulders, so rolling them was hard, and pushing them up an incline took an enormous effort. The youngest brother quit first. He said, 'Brothers, this place is good enough for me. It's close to the shore, and I can catch fish. It has everything I need to go on living. I don't mind if I can't see that much of the world from here.' His two elder brothers pressed on, but when they were midway up the mountain, the second brother quit. He said, 'Brother, this place is good enough for me. There is plenty of fruit here. It has everything I need to go on living. I don't mind if I can't see that much of the world from here.' The eldest brother continued walking up the mountain. The trail grew increasingly narrow and steep, but he did not quit. He had great powers of perseverance, and he wanted to see as much of the world as he possibly could, so he kept rolling the boulder with all his might. He went on for months, hardly eating or drinking, until he had rolled the boulder to the very peak of the high mountain. There he stopped and surveyed the world. Now he could see more of the world than anyone. This was the place he would live—where no grass grew, where no birds flew. For water, he could only lick the ice and frost. For food, he could only gnaw on moss. Be he had no regrets, because now he could look out over the whole world. And so, even today, his great, round boulder is perched on the peak of that mountain on an island in Hawaii. That's how the story goes."

Silence.

Mari asks, "Is it supposed to have some kind of moral?"

"Two, probably. The first one," he says, holding up a finger, "is that people are all different. Even siblings. And the other one," he says, holding up another finger, "is that if you really want to know something, you have to be willing to pay the price."

Mari offers her opinion: "To me, the lives chosen by the two younger brothers make the most sense."

"True," he concedes. "Nobody wants to go all the way to Hawaii to stay alive licking frost and eating moss. That's for sure. But the eldest brother was curious to see as much of the world as possible, and he couldn't suppress that curiosity, no matter how big the price was he had to pay."

"Intellectual curiosity."

"Exactly."

Mari went on thinking about this for a while, one hand perched on her thick book.

"Even if I asked you very politely what you're reading, you wouldn't tell me, would you?" he asks.

"Probably not."

"It sure looks heavy."

Mari says nothing.

"It's not the size book most girls carry around in their bags."

Mari maintains her silence. He gives up and continues his meal. This time, he concentrates his attention on the chicken salad and finishes it without a word. He takes his time chewing and drinks a lot of water. He asks the waitress to refill his water glass several times. He eats his final piece of toast.

Your house was way out in Hiyoshi, I seem to recall," he says. His empty plates have been cleared away.

Mari nods.

"Then you'll never make the last train. I suppose you can go home by taxi, but the next train's not until tomorrow morning."

"I know that much," Mari says.

"Just checking," he says.

"I don't know where you live, but haven't you missed the last train, too?"

"Not so far: I'm in Koenji. But I live alone, and we're going to be practicing all night. Plus if I really have to get back, my buddy's got a car."

He pats his instrument case like the head of a favorite dog.

"The band practices in the basement of a building near here," he says. "We can make all the noise we want and nobody complains. There's hardly any heat, though, so it gets pretty cold this time of year. But they're letting us use it for free, so we take what we can get."

Mari glances at the instrument case. "That a trombone?"

"That's right! How'd you know?"

"Hell, I know what a trombone looks like."

"Well, sure, but there are tons of girls who don't even know the instrument exists. Can't blame 'em, though. Mick Jagger and Eric Clapton didn't become rock stars playing the trombone. Ever see Jimi Hendrix or Pete Townshend smash a trombone onstage? Of course not. The only thing they smash is electric guitars. If they smashed a trombone, the audience'd laugh."

"So why did you choose the trombone?"

He puts cream in his newly arrived coffee and takes a sip.

"When I was in middle school, I happened to buy a jazz record called *Blues-ette* at a used record store. An old LP. I can't remember why I bought it at the time. I had never heard any jazz before. But anyway, the first tune on side A was 'Five Spot After Dark,' and it was *great*. A guy named Curtis Fuller played the trombone on it. The first time I heard it, I felt the scales fall from my eyes. That's *it*, I thought. *That's* the instrument for me. The trombone and me: it was a meeting arranged by destiny."

The young man hums the first eight bars of "Five Spot After Dark."

"I know that," says Mari.

He looks baffled. "You do?"

Mari hums the next eight bars.

"How do you know that?" he asks.

"Is it against the law for me to know it?"

He sets his cup down and lightly shakes his head. "No, not at all. But, I don't know, it's incredible. For a girl nowadays to know 'Five Spot After Dark' . . . Well, anyway, Curtis Fuller gave me goose bumps, and that got me started playing the trombone. I borrowed money from my parents, bought a used instrument, and joined the school band. Then in high school I started doing different stuff with bands. At first I was backing up a rock band, sort of like the old Tower of Power. Do you know Tower of Power?"

Mari shakes her head.

"It doesn't matter," he says. "Anyhow, that's what I used to do, but now I'm purely into plain, simple jazz. My university's not much of a school, but we've got a pretty good band."

The waitress comes to refill his water glass, but he waves her off. He glances at his watch. "It's time for me to get out of here."

Mari says nothing. Her face says, *Nobody's stopping you.*

"Of course everybody comes late."

Mari offers no comment on that, either.

"Hey, say hi from me to your sister, okay?"

"You can do it yourself, can't you? You know our phone number. How can I say hi from you? I don't even know your name."

He thinks about that for a moment. "Suppose I call your house and Eri Asai answers, what am I supposed to talk about?"

"Get her to help you plan a class reunion, maybe. You'll think of something."

"I'm not much of a talker. Never have been."

"I'd say you've been talking a lot to me."

"With you, I can talk, somehow."

"With me, you can talk, *somehow*," she parrots him. "But with my sister, you can't talk?"

"Probably not."

"Because of too much intellectual curiosity?"

I wonder, says his vague expression. He starts to say something, changes his mind, and stops. He takes a deep breath. He picks up the bill from the table and begins calculating the money in his head.

"I'll leave what I owe. Can you pay for us both later?"

Mari nods.

He glances first at her and then at her book. After a moment's indecision he says, "I know this is none of my business, but is something wrong? Like, problems with your boyfriend or a big fight with your family? I mean, staying in town alone by yourself all night . . ."

Mari puts on her glasses and stares up at him. The silence between them is tense and chilly. He raises both palms toward her as if to say, *Sorry for butting in.*

"I'll probably be back here around five in the morning for a snack," he says. "I'll be hungry again. I hope I see you then."

"Why?"

"Hmm, I wonder why."

"'Cause you're worried about me?"

"That's part of it."

"'Cause you want me to say hi to my sister?"

"That might be a little part of it, too."

"My sister wouldn't know the difference between a trombone and a toaster oven. She could tell the difference between a Gucci and a Prada at a glance, though, I'm pretty sure."

"Everybody's got their own battlefields," he says with a smile.

He takes a notebook from his coat pocket and writes something in it with a ballpoint pen. He tears the page out and hands it to her.

"This is the number of my cell phone. Call me if any-thing happens. Uh, do *you* have a cell phone?"

Mari shakes her head.

"I didn't think so," he says as if impressed. "I sorta had this gut feeling, like, 'I'll bet she doesn't like cell phones.' "

The young man stands and puts on his leather coat. He picks up his trombone case. A hint of his smile still remains as he says, "See ya."

Mari nods, expressionless. Without really looking at the scrap of paper, she places it on the table next to the bill. She holds her breath for a moment, props her chin on her hand, and goes back to her book. Burt Bacharach's "The April Fools" plays through the restaurant at low volume.

0 p.m.

2

The room is dark, but our eyes gradually adjust to the darkness. A woman lies in bed, asleep. A young, beautiful woman: Mari's sister, Eri. Eri Asai. We know this without having been told so by anyone. Her black hair cascades across the pillow like a flood of dark water.

We allow ourselves to become a single point of view, and we observe her for a time. Perhaps it should be said that we are peeping in on her. Our viewpoint takes the form of a midair camera that can move freely about the room. At the moment, the camera is situated directly above the bed and is focused on her sleeping face. Our angle changes at intervals as regular as the blinking of an eye. Her small, well-shaped lips are tightened into a straight line. At first glance, we can discern no sign of breathing, but staring hard we can make out a slight—a very slight—movement at the base of her throat. She *is* breathing. She lies with her head on the pillow as if looking up at the ceiling. She is not, in fact, looking at anything. Her eyelids are closed like hard winter buds. Her sleep is deep. She is probably not even dreaming.

As we observe Eri Asai, we gradually come to sense
that there is something about her sleep that is *not normal.*
It is too pure, too perfect. Not a muscle in her face, not
an eyelash moves. Her slender white neck preserves the
dense tranquility of a handcrafted product. Her small
chin traces a clean angle like a well-shaped headland.
Even in the profoundest somnolence, people do not tread
so deeply into the realm of sleep. They do not attain such
a total surrender of consciousness.

But consciousness—or its absence—is of no concern as
long as the functions for sustaining life are maintained.
Eri's pulse and respiration continue at the lowest possible level. Her existence seems to have been placed upon
the narrow threshold that separates the organic from the
inorganic—secretly, and with great care. How or why this
condition was brought about we as yet have no way of
knowing. Eri Asai is in a deep, deliberate state of sleep as
if her entire body has been enveloped in warm wax.
Clearly, something here is incompatible with nature. This
is all we can conclude for now.

The camera draws back slowly to convey an image of
the entire room. Then it begins observing details in
search of clues. This is by no means a highly decorated
room. Neither is it a room that suggests the tastes or individuality of its occupant. Without detailed observation, it
would be hard to tell that this was the room of a young girl.
There are no dolls, stuffed animals, or other accessories
to be seen. No posters or calendars. On the side facing
the window, one old wooden desk and a swivel chair. The
window itself is covered by a roll-down window shade. On

the desk is a simple black lamp and a brand-new note-book computer (its top closed). A few ballpoint pens and pencils in a mug.

By the wall stands a plain wood-framed single bed, and there sleeps Eri Asai. The bedclothes are solid white. On shelves attached to the opposite wall, a compact stereo and a small pile of CDs in their cases. Next to those, a phone. A dresser with mirror attached. The only things placed in front of the mirror are lip balm and a small, round hairbrush. On that wall is a walk-in closet. As the room's only decorative touch, five photographs in small frames are lined up on a shelf, all of them photos of Eri Asai. She is alone in all of them. None show her with friends or family. They are professional photographs of her posing as a model, photos that might have appeared in magazines. There is a small bookcase, but it contains only a handful of books, mostly college textbooks. And a pile of large-size fashion magazines. It would be hard to conclude that she is a voracious reader.

Our point of view, as an imaginary camera, picks up and lingers over things like this in the room. We are invis-ible, anonymous intruders. We look. We listen. We note odors. But we are not physically present in the place, and we leave behind no traces. We follow the same rules, so to speak, as orthodox time travelers. We observe but we do not intervene. Honestly speaking, however, the infor-mation regarding Eri Asai that we can glean from the appearance of this room is far from abundant. It gives the impression that preparations have been made to hide her personality and cleverly elude observing eyes.

Near the head of the bed a digital clock soundlessly

and steadily renews its display of the time. For now, the clock is the only thing in the room evidencing anything like movement: a cautious nocturnal creature that runs on electricity. Each green crystal numeral slips into the place of another, evading human eyes. The current time is 11:59 p.m.

Once it has finished examining individual details, our viewpoint camera draws back momentarily and surveys the room once again. Then, as if unable to make up its mind, it maintains its broadened field of vision, its line of sight fixed in place for the time being. A pregnant silence reigns. At length, however, as if struck by a thought, it turns toward—and begins to approach—a television set in a corner of the room: a perfectly square black Sony. The screen is dark, and as dead as the far side of the moon, but the camera seems to have sensed some kind of presence there—or perhaps a kind of foreshadowing. Wordlessly, we share this presence or foreshadowing with the camera as we stare at the screen in close-up.

We wait. We hold our breath and listen.

The clock displays "0:00."

We hear a faint electrical crackling, and a hint of life crosses the TV screen as it begins to flicker almost imperceptibly. Could someone have entered the room and turned on the switch without our noticing? Could a preset timer have come on? But no: our ever-alert camera circles to the back of the device and reveals that the television's plug has been pulled. Yes, the TV should, in fact, be dead. It should, in fact, be cold and hard as it presides over the silence of midnight. Logically. Theoretically. But it is not dead.

Scan lines appear, flicker, break up, and vanish. Then the lines come to the surface of the screen again. The faint crackling continues without letup. Eventually the screen begins to display something. An image begins taking shape. Soon, however, it becomes diagonally deformed, like italics, and disappears like a flame blown out. Then the whole process starts again. The image strains to right itself. Trembling, it tries to give concrete form to something. But the image will not come together. It distorts as if the TV's antenna is being blown by a strong wind. Then it breaks apart and scatters. Every phase of this turmoil is conveyed to us by the camera.

The sleeping woman appears to be totally unaware of these events occurring in her room. She evidences no response to the outpouring of light and sound from the TV set but goes on sleeping soundly amid an established completeness. For now, nothing can disturb her deep sleep. The television is a new intruder into the room. We, too, are intruders, of course, but unlike us, the new intruder is neither quiet nor transparent. Nor is it neutral. It is undoubtedly *trying to intervene*. We sense its intention intuitively.

The TV image comes and goes, but its stability slowly increases. On-screen is the interior of a room. A fairly big room. It could be a space in an office building, or some kind of classroom. It has a large plate-glass window; banks of fluorescent lights line the ceiling. There is no sign of furniture, however. No, on closer inspection there is exactly one chair set in the middle of the room. An old wooden chair, it has a back but no arms. It is a practical chair, and very plain. Someone is sitting in it. The picture has not stabilized entirely, and so we can make out the person in the chair only as a vague silhouette with blurred outlines. The room has the chilling air of a place that has been long abandoned.

The camera that seems to be conveying this image to the television cautiously approaches the chair. The build of the person in the chair seems to be that of a man. He is leaning forward slightly. He faces the camera and appears to be deep in thought. He wears dark clothing and leather shoes. We can't see his face, but he seems to be a rather thin man of medium height. It is impossible to tell his age. As we gather these fragments of information from the unclear screen, the image breaks up every now and then. The interference undulates and rises. Not for long, however: the image soon recovers. The static also quiets down. Without a doubt the screen is moving toward stability.

Something is about to happen in this room. Something of great significance.

3

*T*he interior of the same Denny's as before. Martin Denny's "More" is playing in the background. The number of customers has decreased markedly from thirty minutes earlier, and there are no more voices raised in conversation. The atmosphere suggests a deeper stage of night.

Mari is still at her table, reading her thick book. In front of her sits a plate containing a vegetable sandwich, virtually untouched. She seems to have ordered it less out of hunger than as a means to buy herself more time at the restaurant. Now and then she changes the position in which she reads her book—resting her elbows on the table, or settling farther back into her seat. Sometimes she raises her face, takes a deep breath, and checks out the restaurant's dwindling occupancy, but aside from this she maintains her concentration on her book. Her ability to concentrate seems to be one of her most important personal assets.

There are more single customers to be seen now: someone writing on a laptop, someone text-messaging on a cell phone, another absorbed in reading like Mari, another doing nothing but staring thoughtfully out the window. Maybe they can't sleep. Maybe they don't want to sleep. A family restaurant provides such people with a place to park themselves late at night.

A large woman charges in as if she could hardly wait for the restaurant's automatic glass door to open. She is solidly constructed, not fat. Her shoulders are broad and strong-looking. She wears a black woolen hat pulled down to the eyes, a big leather jacket, and orange pants. Her hands are empty. Her powerful appearance draws people's attention. As soon as she comes in, a waitress asks her, "Table for one, ma'am?" but the woman ignores her and casts anxious eyes around the restaurant. Spotting Mari, she takes long strides in her direction.

When she arrives at Mari's table, she says nothing but immediately lowers herself into the seat across from Mari. For a woman so large, her movements are quick and efficient.

"Uh . . . mind?" she asks.

Mari, who has been concentrating on her book, looks up. Finding this large stranger sitting opposite her, she is startled.

The woman pulls off her woolen hat. Her hair is an intense blond, and it is cut as short as a well-trimmed lawn. Her face wears an open expression, but the skin has a tough, weathered look, like long-used rainwear, and although the features are not exactly symmetrical, there is something reassuring about them that seems to come from an innate fondness for people. Instead of introducing herself, she gives Mari a lopsided smile and rubs her thick palm over her short blond hair.

The waitress comes and tries to set a glass of water and a menu on the table as called for in the Denny's training manual, but the woman waves her away. "Never mind, I'm getting outta here right away. Sorry, hon."

The waitress responds with a nervous smile and leaves.

"You're Mari Asai, right?" the woman asks.

"Well, yes . . ."

"Takahashi said you'd probably still be here."

"Takahashi?"

"Tetsuya Takahashi. Tall guy, long hair, skinny. Plays trombone."

Mari nods. "Oh, him."

"Yeah. He says you speak fluent Chinese."

"Well," Mari answers cautiously, "I'm okay with everyday conversation. I'm not exactly fluent."

"That's fine. Can I getcha to come with me? I've got this Chinese girl in a mess. She can't speak Japanese, so I don't know what the hell is going on."

Mari had no idea what the woman was talking about, but she set a bookmark in place, closed the book, and pushed it aside.

"What kind of mess?"

"She's kinda hurt. Close by. An easy walk. I won't take much of your time. I just need you to translate for her and give me some idea what happened. I'd really appreciate it."

Mari has a moment of hesitation, but, looking at her face, she guesses that the woman is not a bad person. She slips her book into her shoulder bag and puts on her jacket. She reaches for the bill on the table, but the woman beats her to it.

"I'll pay this."

"That's all right. It's stuff I ordered."

"Never mind, it's the least I can do. Just shut up and let me pay."

When they stand up, the difference in their sizes becomes obvious. Mari is a tiny girl, and the woman is built like a barn, maybe two or three inches shy of six feet. Mari gives up and lets the woman pay for her.

They step outside. The street is as busy as ever despite the time. Electronic sounds from the game center. Shouts of karaoke club barkers. Motorcycle engines roaring. Three young men sit on the pavement outside a shuttered shop doing nothing in particular. When Mari and the woman pass by, the three look up and follow them with their eyes, probably wondering about this odd couple, but saying nothing, just staring. The shutter is covered with spray-painted graffiti.

"My name's Kaoru," the woman says. "Yeah, I know, you're thinking, 'How did this big hunk of a woman get a pretty little name like that?' But I've been Kaoru ever since I was born."

"Glad to meet you," Mari says.

"Sorry for dragging you out like this. Bet I threw you for a loop."

Mari doesn't know how to respond, and so she says nothing.

"Want me to carry your bag? Looks heavy," Kaoru says.

"I'm okay."

"What's in there?"

"Books, a change of clothes . . ."

"You're not a runaway, are you?"

"No, I'm not," says Mari.

"Okay. Good."

The two keep walking. From the brightly lighted avenue they turn into a narrow lane and head uphill. Kaoru walks quickly and Mari hurries to keep pace with her. They climb a gloomy, deserted stairway and come out to a different street. The stairs seem to be a shortcut between the two streets. Several snack bars on this street still have their signs lighted, but none of them suggests a human presence.

"It's that love ho over there."

"Love ho?"

"Love hotel. For couples. By the hour. See the neon sign, 'Alphaville'? That's it."

When she hears the name, Mari can't help staring at Kaoru. "Alphaville?"

"Don't worry. It's okay. I'm the manager."

"The injured woman is in there?"

Walking on, Kaoru turns and says, "Uh-huh. It's kinda hard to explain."

"Is Takahashi in there, too?"

"No, he's in another building near here. In the basement. His band's practicing all night. Students have it easy."

The two walk in through the front door of the Alphaville. Guests at this hotel choose their room from large photos on display in the foyer, press the corresponding numbered button, receive their key, and take the elevator straight to the room. No need to meet or talk to anyone. Room charges come in two types: "rest" and "overnight." Gloomy blue illumination. Mari takes in all these new sights. Kaoru says a quiet hello to the woman at the reception desk in back.

Then she says to Mari, "You've probably never been in a place like this before."

"No, this is the first time for me."

"Oh, well, there are lots of different businesses in the world."

Kaoru and Mari take the elevator to the top floor. Down a short, narrow corridor they come to a door numbered 404. Kaoru gives two soft knocks and the door opens instantly inward. A young woman with hair dyed a bright red nervously pokes her head out. She is thin and pale. She wears an oversize pink T-shirt and jeans with holes. Large earrings hang from her pierced ears.

"Oh, cool, it's you, Kaoru!" says the red-haired young woman. "Took you long enough. I was going crazy."

"How's she doing?"

"Same old same old."

"The bleeding stop?"

"Pretty much. I used a ton of paper towels, though."

Kaoru lets Mari in and closes the door. Besides the red-haired woman there is another employee in the room, a small woman who wears her hair up and is mopping the floor. Kaoru does a quick introduction.

"This is Mari. The one who can speak Chinese. The redhead here is Komugi. Yeah, I *know* it sounds like 'Wheat,' but it's the name her parents gave her, so what're ya gonna do? She's been working for me forever."

Komugi produces a nice smile for Mari and says, "Glad to meet ya."

"Glad to meet you," says Mari.

"The other one over there is Korogi. Now, that's *not* her real name. You'll have to ask her why she wants to be known as 'Cricket.'"

"Sorry about that," says Korogi in the soft tones of the Kansai region around Osaka. "I got rid of my real name." Korogi looks a few years older than Komugi.

"Glad to meet you," says Mari.

The room is windowless and stuffy and all but filled with the oversize bed and TV. Crouching on the floor in one corner is a naked woman in a bath towel. She hides her face in her hands and cries soundlessly. Blood-soaked towels lie on the floor. The bedsheets are also bloody. A floor lamp lies where it was knocked down. On the table is a half-empty bottle of beer and one glass. The TV is on and tuned to a comedy show. The audience laughs. Kaoru picks up the remote and switches it off.

"Looks like he beat the crap out of her," she says to Mari.

"The man she was here with?" Mari asks.

"Uh-huh. Her customer."

"Customer? She's a prostitute?"

"Yeah, we mostly get pros at this time of night," Kaoru says. "So sometimes we have problems. Like they fight over the money, or the guy wants some perverted stuff or something."

Mari bites her lip and tries to gather her thoughts. "And she only speaks Chinese?"

"Yeah, she knows like two words of Japanese. I can't call the cops, though. She's probably an illegal alien, and I don't have time to go testify every time something like this comes up."

Mari sets her shoulder bag on the table and goes to the crouching woman. She kneels down and speaks to her in Chinese:

"*Ni zenme le?*" (What happened?)

The woman may not have heard her. She doesn't answer. Shoulders quaking, she sobs uncontrollably.

Kaoru shakes her head. "She's in some kind of shock. I bet he really hurt her."

Mari speaks to the woman again. "*Shi Zhongguoren ma?*" (Are you from China?)

Still the woman does not answer.

"*Fangxin ba, wo gen jingcha mei guanxi.*" (Don't worry, I'm not with the police.)

Still the woman does not answer.

"*Ni bei ta da le ma?*" (Did a man beat you up?)

The woman finally nods. Her long black hair trembles.

Mari continues speaking, quietly but persistently, to the woman. She asks the same question several times. Kaoru folds her arms and watches their interaction with a worried look. Komugi and Korogi, meanwhile, share the cleanup duties. They gather the bloody paper towels and stuff them in a vinyl trash bag. They strip the bed and put fresh towels in the bathroom. They raise the lamp from the floor and take away the beer bottle and glass. They check replaceable items and clean the bathroom. The two are obviously accustomed to working together. Their movements are smooth and economical.

Mari goes on kneeling in the corner, speaking to the woman, who seems to have calmed down somewhat at the sound of the familiar language. Haltingly, she explains the situation to Mari in Chinese. Her voice is so faint,

Mari has to lean close to her in order to hear. She listens intently, nodding. Now and then she says a phrase or two as if to encourage the woman.

Kaoru gives Mari's shoulder a little tap from behind. "Sorry, but we need this room for the next customer. We're gonna take her to the office downstairs. Come along, okay?"

"But she's completely naked! She says he took everything she had on. Shoes, underwear, everything."

Kaoru shakes her head. "He stripped her clean so she couldn't report him right away. What a bastard!"

Kaoru takes a thin bathrobe from the closet and hands it to Mari. "Just get her to put this on for now."

The woman rises weakly to her feet and, looking half-stunned, drops the towel, exposing her nakedness as she puts on the robe, her stance unsteady. Mari quickly averts her gaze. The woman's body is small but beautiful: well-shaped breasts, smooth skin, a shadowy hint of pubic hair. She is probably the same age as Mari, her build still girlish. Her steps are uncertain. Kaoru puts a supporting arm around her shoulders and leads her from the room. They take a service elevator down, Mari following with her bag. Komugi and Korogi stay behind to clean the room.

*T*he three women enter the hotel office. Cardboard cartons are piled along the walls. One steel desk and a simple reception area with couch and armchair. On the desk are a computer keyboard and a glowing liquid crystal monitor. On the walls hang a calendar, a framed piece of pop calligraphy by Mitsuo Aida, and an electric clock. There is a portable TV, and on top of a small refrigerator stands a

microwave oven. The room feels cramped with three people in it. Kaoru guides the bathrobed Chinese prostitute
to the couch. The woman seems cold as she clutches at
the bathrobe, drawing it closed.

Kaoru aims the light of the floor lamp at the prostitute's
face and examines her wounds more closely. She brings
over a first-aid kit and carefully wipes away the dried
blood with alcohol and cotton swabs. She puts Band-Aids
on the cuts. She feels the woman's nose to see if it is
broken. She lifts her eyelids and checks to see how badly
bloodshot the eyes are. She runs her fingers over the
woman's head, feeling for bumps. She performs these
tasks with amazing deftness, as if she does them all the
time. She takes some kind of cold pack from the refrigerator, wraps it in a small towel, and hands it to the woman.

"Here, press this against your face for a while."

Recalling that her listener understands no Japanese,
Kaoru shows her with gestures where to put it. The
woman nods and presses the cold pack under her eyes.

Kaoru turns to Mari and says, "That was some pretty
spectacular bleeding, but it was mostly from the nose.
Luckily, she doesn't have any big wounds, no bumps on
her head, and I don't think her nose is broken. She's cut at
the corner of her eye and on the lip, but nothing that
needs stitches. She'll probably be out of business for a
week with black eyes."

Mari nods.

"The guy was strong, but he's obviously a total amateur
when it comes to beating somebody up. He just threw a
lot of wild punches. I'll bet his hands are killing him now,
the bastard. He swung so hard he dented the wall in a few

places. He really lost it. He didn't know what he was doing."

Komugi comes in and takes something from one of the cartons piled against the wall—a fresh bathrobe to replace the one from room 404.

Mari says, "She told me he took everything—her pocketbook, her money, her cell phone."

"Just so he could skip out without paying her?" Komugi interjects.

"No, not that. I mean . . . her, uh, period started all of a sudden before they could do anything. It was early. So he got mad and . . ."

"Well, *she* couldn't help it," says Komugi. "When it starts, it starts—bang!"

Kaoru clucks and says, "Okay, that's enough from you, Komugi. Go finish cleaning 404."

"Yes, ma'am. Sorry," Komugi says and leaves the office.

"So he's all set to do it, the woman gets her period, he goes crazy, beats the shit out of her, grabs her money and clothes, and gets the hell out of there," Kaoru says. "That guy's got problems."

Mari nods. "She says she's sorry for getting the sheets all bloody."

"That's okay, we're used to it," Kaoru says. "I don't know why, but lots of girls' periods start in love hos. They're always calling downstairs and asking for napkins 'n' tampons 'n' stuff. I wanna say, 'What are we—a drugstore?' But anyhow, we've gotta get this kid dressed. She's not goin' anywhere like this."

Kaoru searches in another carton and pulls out a pair of panties in a vinyl pack—the kind used in vending machines in the rooms. "These are cheapies for emergencies. They can't be laundered, but let her put on a pair. We don't want her to have any drafts down there making her nervous."

Next Kaoru hunts in the closet and comes out with a faded-green jersey top and bottom she hands to the prostitute.

"These belonged to a girl who used to work here. Don't worry, they're clean. She doesn't have to give them back. All I've got is rubber flip-flops for her feet, but that'll be better than nothing."

Mari explains this to the woman. Kaoru opens a cabinet and takes out a few sanitary napkins. She hands them to the prostitute.

"Use these, too. You can change in that bathroom." She motions toward the door with her chin.

The prostitute nods and thanks her in Japanese: *"Arigato."* Then she takes the clothing into the bathroom.

Kaoru lowers herself into the desk chair, shakes her head slowly, and says, "You never know what's gonna happen in this business."

"She tells me it's just over two months since she came to Japan," Mari says.

"She's here illegally, I suppose?"

"I didn't ask her about that. Judging from her dialect, she's from the north."

"Old Manchuria?"

"Probably."

"Huh. I suppose somebody's gonna come and pick her up."

"I think she's got a boss of some kind."

"A Chinese gang," Kaoru says. "They run prostitution around here. They sneak women in by boat from the mainland and make them pay for it with their bodies. They take phone orders and deliver the women to hotels on motorcycles—hot 'n' fresh, like pizza. They're one of our best clients."

"By 'gang,' you mean like yakuza?"

Kaoru shakes her head. "No, no. I was a professional wrestler a long time, and we used to do these national tours, so I got to know a few yakuza. Let me tell you, compared to these Chinese gangsters, Japanese yakuza are sweethearts. I mean, you never know what's coming with them. But this kid's got no choice: if she doesn't go back to them, she's got no place to go."

"Do you think they're going to be hard on her for not making anything this time?"

"Hmm, I wonder. With her face looking like that, it'll be a while before she can have any customers, and she's worthless to them if she can't make money. She's a pretty thing, though."

The prostitute comes out of the bathroom wearing the jersey outfit and rubber thongs. The top has an Adidas logo on the chest. The bruises remain distinct on the woman's face, but her hair is now more neatly combed. Even in this well-worn outfit and with her lips swollen and face bruised, she is a beautiful woman.

Kaoru asks her in Japanese, "I'll bet you want to use the phone, right?"

Mari translates into Chinese. *"Yao da dianhua ma?"* Would you like to use the telephone?

The prostitute answers in fragmented Japanese. *"Hai. Arigato."*

Kaoru hands her a white cordless phone. She presses the buttons and, speaking softly in Chinese, she makes a report to the person on the other end, who responds with an angry outburst. She gives a short answer and hangs up. With a grim expression, she hands the phone back to Kaoru.

The prostitute thanks Kaoru in Japanese: *"Domo arigato."* Then she turns to Mari and says, *"Mashang you ren lai jie wo."* (Someone is coming to pick me up. Right away.)

Mari explains to Kaoru: "I think they're coming to get her now."

Kaoru frowns. "Come to think of it, the hotel bill hasn't been paid, either. Usually the man pays, but this particular son-of-a-bitch left without paying. He owes us for a beer, too."

"Are you going to get it from the one who picks her up?"

"Hmm." Kaoru stops to think this over. "I hope it's that simple."

Kaoru puts tea leaves in a pot followed by hot water from a thermos jar. She pours the tea into three cups and hands one to the Chinese prostitute. The woman thanks her and takes a drink. The hot tea hurts her cut lip. She takes one sip and furrows her brow.

Kaoru drinks some tea and says to the prostitute in Japanese, "But it's hard for you, isn't it? You come all the way from China, sneak into Japan, and you end up with those goons sucking the life outta you. I don't know what it was like for you back home, but you probably would've been better off not coming here, don't you think?"

"You want me to translate that?" Mari asks.

Kaoru shakes her head. "Nah, why bother? I'm just talking to myself."

Mari engages the prostitute in conversation. *"Ni ji sui le?"* (How old are you?)

"Shijiu." (Nineteen.)

"Wo ye shi. Jiao shenme mingzi?" (Same as me. What's your name?)

The prostitute hesitates a moment and answers, "Guo Dongli."

"Wo jiao Mali." (My name is Mari.)

Mari offers the woman a little smile—her first since midnight.

A motorcycle comes to a halt at the front entrance of the Alphaville: a big, tough-looking Honda sports bike. The man driving it wears a full-face helmet. He leaves the engine running as though he wants to be ready to get out fast if he has to. He wears a tight-fitting black leather jacket and blue jeans. High-top basketball shoes. Thick gloves. The man takes off his helmet and sets it on the gas tank. After a careful scan of his surroundings, he takes off one glove, pulls a cell phone from his pocket, and punches in a number. He is around thirty. Reddish dyed hair, ponytail. Broad forehead, sunken cheeks, sharp eyes. After a short conversation, the man hangs up and puts the phone back into his pocket. He pulls his glove back on and waits.

Soon Kaoru, the prostitute, and Mari step outside.

Rubber sandals flapping, the prostitute drags herself toward the motorcycle. The temperature has fallen, and she seems cold in her jersey outfit. The motorcycle man barks something at the prostitute, who responds softly.

Kaoru says to the motorcycle man, "Ya know, fella, I still haven't been paid for my hotel room."

The man stares hard at Kaoru, then says, "I don't pay hotel bills. The john pays." His speech is flat, unaccented, expressionless.

"I know that," Kaoru says in a hoarse voice. She clears her throat. "But think about it. You scratch my back, I scratch yours. That's how we do business. This has been a drag for us, too. I mean, this was a case of assault with bodily injury. We could've called the cops. But then you guys would've had a little explaining to do, right? So just pay us our sixty-eight hundred yen and we'll be satisfied. Won't even charge you for the beer. Call it even."

The man stares at Kaoru with expressionless eyes. He looks up at the neon sign: Alphaville. He takes off a glove again, pulls a leather billfold from his jacket pocket, counts out seven thousand-yen bills, and lets them drop to his feet. There is no wind: the bills lie flat on the ground. The man puts his glove back on. He raises his arm and looks at his watch. He performs each movement with unnatural slowness. He is clearly in no hurry. He seems to be trying to impress the three women with the sheer weight of his presence. He can take as much time as he likes for anything. All the while, the motorcycle engine keeps up its deep rumbling, like a skittish animal.

"You're pretty gutsy," the man says to Kaoru.

"Thanks," Kaoru answers.

"If you call the cops there might be a fire in the neigh-borhood," he says.

A deep silence reigns for a time. Arms folded, Kaoru keeps her eyes locked on the man's face. Her own face marked with cuts, the prostitute looks uneasily from one to the other, unable to comprehend their give-and-take.

Eventually the man picks up his helmet, slips it on, beckons to the woman, and seats her on his motorcycle. She holds on to his jacket with both hands. Turning, she looks back at Mari and at Kaoru. Then she looks at Mari again. She seems to want to speak but finally says nothing. The man gives the pedal a strong kick, revs the engine, and drives off. The sound of his exhaust reverberates heavily through the midnight streets. Kaoru and Mari are left standing there. Kaoru bends over and picks up the thousand-yen bills one at a time. She turns them so they face the same way, folds the wad in half, and stuffs it into her pocket. She takes a deep breath and rubs her palm over her short blond hair.

"Man!" she says.

O. a.m.

4

Eri Asai's room.

Nothing has changed. The image of the man in the chair, however, is larger than before. Now we can see him fairly clearly. The signal is still experiencing some interference: at times the image wavers, its outlines bend, its quality fades, and static rises. Now and then a completely unrelated image intrudes momentarily. But the jumble subsides, and the original image returns.

Eri Asai is still sound asleep in the bed. The artificial glow of the television screen produces moving shadows on her profile but does not disturb her sleep.

The man on the screen wears a dark brown business suit. The suit may well have been an impressive article of clothing in its day, but now it is clearly worn out. Patches of something like white dust cling to the sleeves and back. The man wears black, round-toed shoes which are also smudged with dust. He seems to have arrived at this room after passing through a place with deep piles of dust. He wears a standard dress shirt and plain black woolen tie, both of which share that look of fatigue. His hair is tinged with gray. No, it just may be that his black hair is splotched with the white dust. In any case, it has not been properly combed for a long time. Strangely, however, the man's appearance gives no impression of poor grooming, no sense of shabbiness. He is just tired—profoundly exhausted—after unavoidable circumstances have conspired to smear him, suit and all, with dust.

We cannot see his face. For now, the TV camera captures only his back or parts of his body other than his face. Whether because of the angle of the light or through some deliberate arrangement, the face is always in a place of dark shadow inaccessible to our eyes.

The man does not move. Every now and then he takes a long, deep breath and his shoulders slowly rise and fall. He could be a hostage who has been confined to a single room for a very long time. Hovering around him there seems to be a drawn-out sense of resignation. Not that he is tied to the chair: he just sits there with his back straight, breathing quietly, staring at one spot directly in front of him. We cannot tell by looking at him whether he has decided for himself that he will not move or he has been placed into some kind of situation that does not permit him to move. His hands rest on his knees. The time is unclear. We cannot even tell if it is night or day. In the light of the banked fluorescent lamps, however, the room is as bright as a summer afternoon.

Eventually the camera circles around to the front and shows his face, but this does not help us to identify him. The mystery only deepens. His entire face is covered by a translucent mask. Perhaps we should not call it a mask: it clings so closely to his face, it is more like a piece of plastic wrap. But, thin as it is, it still serves its purpose as a

mask. While reflecting the light that strikes it as a pale lus-
ter, it never fails to conceal the man's features and expression. The best we can do is surmise the general contours
of his face. The mask has no holes for the nose, mouth, or
eyes, but still it does not seem to prevent him from
breathing or seeing or hearing. Perhaps it has outstanding
breathability or permeability, but, viewing it from the outside, we cannot tell what kind of material or technology
has been used to make it. The mask possesses equal levels
of sorcery and functionality. It has been both handed
down from ancient times with darkness and sent back
from the future with light.

What makes the mask truly eerie is that even though it
fits the face like a second skin, it prevents us from even
imagining what (if anything) the person within is thinking,
feeling, or planning. Is the man's presence a good thing?
A bad thing? Are his thoughts straight? Twisted? Is the
mask meant to hide him? Protect him? We have no clue.
His face covered by this precision-crafted, anonymous
mask, the man sits quietly in the chair being captured by
the television camera, and this gives rise to a situation. All
we can do, it seems, is defer judgment and accept the situation as it is. We shall call him the Man with No Face.

The camera angle is now fixed. It views the Man with
No Face straight on, from just below center. In his brown
suit, he stays perfectly motionless, looking from his side
of the picture tube, through the glass, into *this side*. He
is on the *other side*, looking straight into this room where
we are. Of course his eyes are hidden behind the mysterious glossy mask, but we can vividly feel the existence—
the weight—of his line of vision. With unwavering

determination, he stares at something ahead of him. Judging from the angle of his face, he could well be staring toward Eri Asai's bed. We trace this hypothetical line of vision with great care. Yes, there can be no doubt about it. What the man in the mask is staring at with his invisible eyes is the sleeping form of Eri. It finally dawns on us: this is what he has been doing all along. He is able to see through to this side. The television screen is functioning as a window on this room.

Now and then the picture flickers and recovers. The static also increases. The noise sounds like an amplified sonic version of someone's brain waves. It rises with increasing density, but at a certain point it peaks, begins to degrade, and eventually dies out. Then, as if changing its mind, it emerges again. The same thing repeats. But the line of vision of the Man with No Face never wavers. His concentration is never broken.

A beautiful girl sleeping on and on in bed. Her straight black hair spreads over the pillow like a deeply meaningful fan. Softly pursed lips. Heart and mind at the bottom of the sea. Whenever the TV screen flickers, the light striking her profile wavers, and shadows dance like inscrutable signals. Sitting on a plain wooden chair and staring at her in silence, the Man with No Face. His shoulders rise and fall unobtrusively in concert with his breathing, like an empty boat bobbing on gentle early-morning waves.

In the room, nothing else moves.

a.m.

5

Mari and Kaoru walk down a deserted back street. Kaoru is seeing Mari somewhere. Mari has her navy blue Boston Red Sox cap pulled down low. In the cap, she looks like a boy—which is probably why she always has it with her.

"Man, am I glad you were there," Kaoru says. "I didn't know what the hell was going on."

They descend the same stairway shortcut they climbed on the way to the hotel.

"Hey, let's stop off at a place I know—if you've got the time," Kaoru says.

"Place?"

"I could really use a nice cold beer. How about you?"

"I can't drink."

"So have some juice or something. What the hell, you've gotta be *someplace* killing time till morning."

*T*hey are seated at the counter of a small bar, the only customers. An old Ben Webster record is playing. "My Ideal." From the fifties. Some forty or fifty old-style LPs are lined up on a shelf. Kaoru is drinking draft beer from a tall, thin glass. In front of Mari sits a glass of Perrier with lime juice. Behind the bar, the aging bartender is involved in cracking ice.

"She was pretty, though, wasn't she?" Mari says.

"That Chinese girl?"

"Yeah."

"I suppose so. But she won't be pretty for long, living like that. She'll get old and ugly overnight. I've seen tons of them."

"She's nineteen—like me."

"Okay," Kaoru says, munching on a few nuts. "But age doesn't matter. That kind of work takes a lot out of you. You've gotta have stainless-steel nerves. Otherwise you start shootin' up, and you're finished."

Mari says nothing.

"You a college kid?"

"Uh-huh. I'm doing Chinese at the University of Foreign Studies."

"University of Foreign Studies, huh? What're ya gonna do after you graduate?"

"If possible, I'd like to be a freelance translator or interpreter. I don't think I'm suited to a nine-to-five."

"Smart girl."

"Not really. From the time I was little, though, my parents always told me I'd better study hard, because I'm too ugly for anything else."

Kaoru looks at Mari with narrowed eyes. "You're plenty damn cute. It's true: I'm not just saying it to make you feel good. Let 'em get a load of *me* if they wanna see ugly."

Mari gave an uncomfortable little shrug. "My sister's older than me and she is just *amazing* to look at. As long as I can remember they always compared me to her, like, 'How can two sisters be so different?' It's true: I don't stand a chance if you compare me to her. I'm little, my boobs are small, my hair's kinky, my mouth is too big, and I'm nearsighted *and* astigmatic."

Kaoru laughs. "People usually call stuff like that 'individuality.'"

"Yeah, but it's not easy to think that way if people have been telling you you're ugly from the time you're little."

"So you studied hard?"

"Yeah, pretty much. But I never liked the competition for grades. Plus I wasn't good at sports and I couldn't make friends, so the other kids kind of bullied me, and by the time I got to the third grade I couldn't go to school anymore."

"You mean, like a real phobia?" Kaoru asks.

"Uh-huh. I hated school so much, I'd throw up my breakfast and have terrible stomachaches and stuff."

"Wow. I had awful grades, but I didn't mind school all that much. If there was somebody I didn't like, I'd just beat the crap out of them."

Mari smiles. "I wish I could have done that . . ."

"Never mind. It's nothing to be proud of . . . So then what happened?"

"Well, in Yokohama there was this school for Chinese kids. I had a friend in the neighborhood who went there. Half the classes were in Chinese, but they didn't go crazy over grades like in the Japanese schools, and my friend was there, so I was willing to go. My parents were against it, of course, but there was no other way they could get me to go to school."

"You were a stubborn little thing, I bet."

"Maybe so," Mari says.

"So this Chinese school let Japanese kids in?"

"Uh-huh. They didn't have any special requirements or anything."

"But you probably didn't know any Chinese then?"

"None at all. But I was young, and my friend helped me, so I learned right away. It was good: people weren't so driven. I stayed there all through middle school and high school. My parents weren't too happy about it, though. They wanted me to go to some famous prep school and become a doctor or a lawyer or something. They had our roles picked out for us: the elder sister, Snow White; the younger sister, a little genius."

"Your sister is *that* good-looking?"

Mari nods and takes a sip of her Perrier. "She was already modeling for magazines in middle school. You know, those magazines for teenage girls."

"Wow," Kaoru says. "It must be tough having such a gorgeous elder sister. But anyhow, to change the subject, what's a girl like you doing hanging out all night in a place like this?"

"A girl like me?"

"You know what I mean . . . Anybody can see you're a *respectable* sort of girl."

"I just didn't want to go home."

"You had a fight with your family?"

Mari shakes her head. "No, that's not it. I just wanted to be alone for a while someplace other than my house. Until morning."

"Have you done this kind of thing before?"

Mari keeps silent.

Kaoru says, "I guess it's none of my business, but to tell you the truth, this is not the kind of neighborhood where respectable girls ought to be spending the night. It's got some pretty dangerous characters hanging around. I've had a few scary brushes myself. Between the time the last train leaves and the first train arrives, the place changes: it's not the same as in daytime."

Mari picks up her Boston Red Sox hat from the bar and begins fiddling with the visor, thinking. Eventually, she sweeps the thought away and says, gently but firmly, "Sorry, do you mind if we talk about something else?"

Kaoru grabs a few peanuts and pops them into her mouth. "No, that's fine," she says. "Let's talk about something else."

Mari pulls a pack of Camel Filters from her jacket pocket and lights one with a Bic.

"Hey, you smoke!" exclaims Kaoru.

"Once in a while."

"Tell you the truth, it doesn't become you."

Mari reddens but manages a slightly awkward smile.

"Mind if I have one?" Kaoru asks.

"Sure."

Kaoru puts a Camel in her mouth and lights it with Mari's Bic. She does, in fact, look much more natural than Mari smoking.

"Got a boyfriend?"

Mari gives her head a little shake. "I'm not much interested in boys at the moment."

"You like girls better?"

"Not really. I don't know."

Kaoru puffs on her cigarette and listens to music. A hint of fatigue shows on her face now that she is allowing herself to relax.

Mari says, "You know, I've been wanting to ask you. Why do you call your hotel Alphaville?"

"Hmm, I wonder. The boss probably named it. All love hos have these crazy names. I mean, they're just for men and women to come and do their stuff. All you need is a bed and a bathtub. Nobody gives a damn about the name as long as it sounds like a love ho. Why do you ask?"

"*Alphaville* is the title of one of my favorite movies. Jean-Luc Godard."

"Never heard of it."

"Yeah, it's really old. From the sixties."

"That's maybe where they got it. I'll ask the boss next time I see him. What does it mean, though—'Alphaville'?"

"It's the name of an imaginary city of the near future," Mari says. "Somewhere in the Milky Way."

"Oh, science fiction. Like *Star Wars*?"

"No, it's not at all like *Star Wars*. No special effects, no action. It's more conceptual. Black-and-white, lots of dialogue, they show it in art theaters . . ."

"Whaddya mean, 'conceptual'?"

"Well, for example, if you cry in Alphaville, they arrest you and execute you in public."

"Why?"

"'Cause in Alphaville, you're not allowed to have deep feelings. So there's nothing like love. No contradictions, no irony. They do everything according to numerical formulas."

Kaoru wrinkles her brow. "'Irony'?"

"Irony means taking an objective or inverted view of oneself or of someone belonging to oneself and discovering oddness in that."

Kaoru thinks for a moment about Mari's explanation. "I don't really get it," she says. "But tell me: is there sex in this Alphaville place?"

"Yes, there is sex in Alphaville."

"Sex that doesn't need love or irony."

"Right."

Kaoru gives a hearty laugh. "So, come to think of it, Alphaville may be the perfect name for a love ho."

A well-dressed, middle-aged man of small stature comes in and sits at the end of the bar. He orders a cocktail and starts a hushed conversation with the bartender. He seems to be a regular, sitting in his usual seat and ordering his usual drink. He is one of those unidentifiable people who inhabit the city at night.

Mari asks Kaoru, "You said you used to be a professional wrestler?"

"Yeah, for a *long* time. I was always on the big side, and a good fighter, so they scouted me in high school. I went straight into the ring, and played bad girls the whole time with this crazy blond hair and shaved-off eyebrows and a red scorpion tattoo on my shoulder. I was on TV sometimes, too. I had matches in Hong Kong and Taiwan and stuff, and a kind of local fan club—a small one. I guess you don't watch lady wrestlers?"

"I never have."

"Yeah, well, that's one hell of a way to make a living, too. I hurt my back and retired when I was twenty-nine. I was a wild woman in the ring, so something like that was bound to happen. I was tough, but everything has its limits. With me, it's a personality thing. I don't know how to do things halfway. I guess I'm a crowd pleaser. They'd start roaring and I'd go crazy and do way more than I needed to. So now I get this twinge in my back whenever we get a few days of rain. Once that gets started, I can't do a thing but lay down all day. I'm a mess."

Kaoru turned her head until the bones in her neck cracked.

"When I was popular I used to pull in the money and I had people crawling all over me, but once I quit there was nothing left. Zip. Where'd all the money go? Well, I built a house for my parents back in Yamagata, so I was a good girl as far as that goes, but the rest went to pay off my younger brother's gambling debts or got used up by relatives I hardly knew, or disappeared into fishy investments that some bank guy came along with. Once that happened, people didn't wanna have anything to do with me. I felt *bad*, like, what the hell have I been doing with myself the past ten years? I'm getting ready to turn thirty and I'm falling apart and I've got nothing in the bank. So I'm wondering what I'm gonna do for the rest of my life when somebody in my fan club puts me in touch with the boss of this house and he says, 'Why not become a manager of a love ho?' Manager? Hell, you can see I'm more like a bouncer or bodyguard."

Kaoru drinks what is left of her beer. Then she looks at her watch.

"Don't you have to get back to work?" Mari asks.

"In a love ho, this is the time you can take it easy. The trains aren't running anymore, so most of the customers now are gonna stay the night, and nothing much will happen till the morning. I guess you can say I'm on duty, but nobody's gonna give me a hard time for drinking a beer."

"So you work all night and then go home?"

"Well, I've got an apartment I can go back to, but there's nothing for me to do there, nobody waiting for me. I spend more nights in the hotel's back room and just start work when I get up. What're *you* gonna do now?"

"Just kill time reading a book somewhere."

"Y'know, you can stay in our place if you don't mind. We can put you up in one of the empty rooms—we've got a few tonight. It's a little sad to spend a night alone in a love ho, but it's great for sleeping. Beds are one thing we've got plenty of."

Mari gives a little nod, but her mind is made up. "Thanks, but I can manage by myself."

"Okay, if you say so."

"Is Takahashi practicing somewhere nearby? His band, I mean."

"Oh yeah, Takahashi. They'll be wailin' away all night in the basement. The building's right down the street. Wanna go have a peek? They're noisy as hell, though."

"No, that's okay. I was just curious."

"Oh, okay. He's a nice kid. He's gonna be something someday. He looks kinda goofy, but he's surprisingly solid underneath. Not bad at all."

"How did you get to know him?"

Kaoru purses her lips out of shape. "Now *that* is an interesting story, but you'd better get it straight from him instead of from me."

Kaoru pays the bill.

"Mari, aren't your folks gonna get mad at you for staying out all night?"

"They think I'm staying at a friend's house. My parents don't worry that much about me, whatever I do."

"I'll bet they think they can leave you alone because you've really got it together."

Mari does not respond to this remark.

"But maybe sometimes you don't really have it together," Kaoru says.

Mari gives her a slight frown. "What makes you think that?"

"It's not a question of what I think. It's part of being nineteen years old. I used to be nineteen myself once. I know what it's like."

Mari looks at Kaoru. She starts to say something, but decides she can't make it come out right, changes her mind.

Kaoru says, "The Skylark is near here. I'll walk you there. The boss is a buddy of mine, so I'm gonna ask him to take care of you. He'll let you stay there till morning. Okay?"

Mari nods. The record ends, the automatic turntable lifts the needle, and the tone arm drops onto its rest. The bartender approaches the player to change records. He carefully lifts the platter and slips it into its jacket. Then he takes out the next record, examines its surface under a light, and sets it on the turntable. He presses a button and the needle descends to the record. Faint scratching. Then Duke Ellington's "Sophisticated Lady" begins to play. Harry Carney's languorous bass clarinet performs solo. The bartender's unhurried movements give the place its own special time flow.

Mari asks the bartender, "Don't you ever play anything but LPs?"

"I don't like CDs," he replies.

"Why not?"

"They're too shiny."

Kaoru butts in to ask the bartender: "Are you a crow?"

"But look at all the time it takes to change LPs," Mari says.

The bartender laughs. "Look, it's the middle of the night. There won't be any trains running till morning. What's the hurry?"

Kaoru cautions Mari, "Remember, this fella's a little on the weird side."

"It's true, though: time moves in its own special way in the middle of the night," the bartender says, loudly striking a book match and lighting a cigarette. "You can't fight it."

"My uncle used to have lots of LPs," Mari says. "Mostly jazz records. He could never get himself to like the sound of CDs. He used to play his stuff for me when I went over there. I was too young to understand the music, but I always liked the smell of old record jackets and the sound of the needle landing in the grooves."

The bartender nods without speaking.

"I learned about Jean-Luc Godard's movies from that same uncle, too," Mari says to Kaoru.

"So, you and your uncle were kinda on the same wavelength, huh?" asks Kaoru.

"Pretty much," Mari says. "He was a professor, but he was kind of a playboy, too. He died all of a sudden three years ago from a heart condition."

The bartender says to Mari, "Stop in any time you like. I open the place at seven every night. Except Sundays."

Mari thanks him and from the counter she picks up a book of the bar's matches, which she stuffs into her jacket pocket. She climbs down from the stool. The sound of the needle tracing the record groove. The languorous, sensual music of Duke Ellington. Music for the middle of the night.

a.m.

*T*he Skylark. Big neon sign. Bright seating area visible through the window. Equally bright laughter from the youthful group of men and women—college students, likely—seated at a large table. This place is far livelier than the Denny's. The deepest darkness of the nighttime streets is unable to penetrate here.

Mari is washing her hands in the Skylark restroom. She is no longer wearing her hat—or her glasses. From a ceiling speaker at low volume an old hit song by the Pet Shop Boys is playing: "Jealousy." Mari's big shoulder bag sits by the sink. She washes her hands with great care, using liquid soap from the dispenser. She appears to be washing off a sticky substance that clings to the spaces between her fingers. Every now and then she looks up at her face

in the mirror. She turns off the water, examines all ten
fingers under the light, and rubs them dry with a paper
towel. She then leans close to the mirror and stares at the
reflection of her face as if she expects something to happen. She doesn't want to miss the slightest change. But
nothing happens. She rests her hands on the sink, closes
her eyes, begins counting, and then opens her eyes again.
Again she examines her face in detail, but still there is no
sign of change.

She straightens her bangs and rearranges the hood of
the parka under her varsity jacket. Then, as if urging herself on, she bites her lip and nods at herself several times.
The Mari in the mirror also bites her lip and nods several
times. She hangs the bag on her shoulder and walks out of
the restroom. The door closes.

Our viewpoint camera lingers in here for a while,
observing the restroom. Mari is no longer here. Neither is
anyone else. Music continues to play from the ceiling
speaker. A Hall and Oates song now: "I Can't Go for
That." A closer look reveals that Mari's image is still
reflected in the mirror over the sink. The Mari in the mirror is looking from her side into this side. Her somber
gaze seems to be expecting some kind of occurrence. But
there is no one on this side. Only her image is left in the
Skylark's restroom mirror.

The room begins to darken. In the deepening darkness, "I Can't Go for That" continues to play.

6

*T*he Hotel Alphaville office. Kaoru sits at the computer looking grumpy. The liquid crystal monitor shows videos taken by the security camera at the front entrance. The image is clear. The time of day is displayed in a corner of the screen. Checking her penciled notes against the time on the monitor, Kaoru uses the mouse to make the image fast-forward and stop. The procedure does not seem to be going well. Now and then she looks at the ceiling and sighs.

Komugi and Korogi walk in.

"Whatcha doin', Kaoru?" Komugi asks.

"Whoa, you sure don't look happy!" Korogi adds.

"Security-camera DVD," Kaoru answers, glaring at the screen. "If I check right around that time, we can probably tell who beat her up."

"But we had all kinds of customers coming and going then. Think we can tell which one did it?" Komugi says.

Kaoru's thick fingers tap clumsily at the keys. "All the other customers were couples, but that guy came alone and waited for the woman in the room. He picked up the key to 404 at 10:52, and she got delivered on the motorcycle ten minutes later. We know that much from Sasaki at the reception desk."

"So all you have to do is look at the frames from ten fifty-two," says Komugi.

"Yeah, but it's not as easy as it sounds," says Kaoru. "I don't know what the hell I'm doing with these digital gizmos."

"Muscles don't help much, do they?" says Komugi.

"You got it."

With an earnest expression, Korogi says, "I think maybe Kaoru was born at the wrong time."

"Yeah," says Komugi. "By like two thousand years."

"Right on," says Korogi.

"Think you've got me all figured out, huh?" says Kaoru. "Can you guys do this stuff?"

"No way!" they chime in together.

Kaoru types the time she wants in the search column and clicks her mouse, but she can't bring up the correct frames. She seems to be performing operations in the wrong sequence. She clucks in frustration. She picks up the manual and flips through it, but can't make sense of it, gives up, and throws it on the desk.

"What the hell am I doing wrong? This ought to bring up the exact frames I want, but it doesn't. I wish to hell Takahashi were here. He'd get it in a split second."

"But still, Kaoru, even if you find out what the guy looks like, what good's it gonna do? You can't report him to the cops," Komugi says.

"I don't go anywhere near the cops if I can help it," says Kaoru. "Not to boast or anything."

"So what're you gonna do?"

"I'll think about that when the time comes," says Kaoru. "It's just the way I'm made: I can't stand by and let a son-of-a-bitch like that pull shit like that. He thinks 'cause he's stronger he can beat up a woman, strip her of everything she's got, and walk away. And on top of it he doesn't pay his damn hotel bill. That's a man for you—a real scumball."

"Somebody oughta catch that fuckin' psycho and beat him half to death," says Korogi.

"Right on," says Kaoru with a vigorous nod. "But he'd never be stupid enough to show his face here again. Not for a while, at least. And who's got time to go looking for him?"

"So what're ya gonna do?" Komugi asks.

"Like I said, I'll think about that when the time comes."

All but punching the mouse in desperation, Kaoru double-clicks on a random icon, and a few seconds later the screen for 10:48 appears on the monitor.

"At last."

Komugi: "If at first you don't succeed . . ."

Korogi: "Betcha scared the computer."

The three of them stare at the screen in silence, holding their breath. A young couple come in at 10:50. Students, probably. Both are obviously tense. They stand in front of the room photos, settling first on one, then another, and finally choosing room 302. They push the button, take the key, and after wandering in search of the elevator, they get on.

Kaoru: "So these're the guests in room three-oh-two."

Komugi: "Three-oh-two, huh? They *look* innocent enough, but they went *wild* in there. You shoulda *seen* the place after they were through with it."

Korogi: "So what? They're young. They pay to come to a place like this so they *can* go wild."

Komugi: "Well, *I'm* still young, but you don't see *me* goin' wild."

Korogi: "That's 'cause you're not horny enough."

Komugi: "Think so? I wonder . . ."

Kaoru: "Hey, here comes number four-oh-four. Shut up and watch."

A man appears on the screen. The time is 10:52.

He wears a light gray trench coat, is in his late thirties, maybe close to forty. He has on a tie and dress shoes like a typical company man. Small wire-frame glasses. He is not carrying anything; his hands are shoved deep into the pockets of his trench coat. Everything about him is ordinary—height, build, hairstyle. If you passed him on the street, he would leave no impression.

"Looks like a totally ordinary guy," says Komugi.

"The ordinary-looking ones are the most dangerous," says Kaoru, rubbing her chin. "They carry around a shit-load of stress."

The man glances at his watch and, without hesitation, takes the key to 404. He strides swiftly toward the elevator, disappearing from the monitor.

Kaoru pauses the image and asks the girls, "So what does this tell us?"

"Looks like a guy from some company," says Komugi.

Kaoru shakes her head, looking at Komugi with apparent disgust. "I don't need *you* to tell me that a guy in a business suit and tie at this time of day has got to be a company guy on his way home from work."

"Sorrreeee," says Komugi.

Korogi offers her opinion: "I'd say he's done this kind of thing a lot. Knows his way around. No hesitation."

"Right on," says Kaoru. "Grabs the key right away and heads straight for the elevator. No wasted motion. No looking around."

Komugi: "You mean this ain't his first time here?"

Korogi: "One of our regular customers, in other words."

Kaoru: "Probably. And he's probably bought his women the same way before, too."

Komugi: "Some guys like to specialize in Chinese women."

Kaoru: "*Lots* of guys. So think about it: he's an office worker and he's been here a few times. There's a good possibility he works in a company around here."

Komugi: "Hey, you're right . . ."

Korogi: "And he works the night shift a lot?"

Kaoru scowls at Korogi. "What gives you that idea? He puts in a day's work, stops off for a beer, starts feelin' good, gets hungry for a woman. That could happen."

Korogi: "Yeah, but this guy wasn't carrying anything. Left his stuff in the office. He'd be carrying something if he was going home—a briefcase or a manila envelope or something. None of these company guys commute empty-handed. Which means this guy was going back to the office for more work. That's what I think."

Komugi: "So he works all night?"

Korogi: "There's a bunch of people like that. They stay at the office and work till morning. Especially computer-software guys. They start messing around with the system after everybody else goes home and there's nobody around. They can't shut the system down while everybody's working, so they stay till two or three in the morning and take a taxi home. The company pays for the cabs with vouchers."

Komugi: "Hey, come to think of it, the guy really *looks* like a computer geek. But how come you know so much, Korogi?"

Korogi: "Well, I wasn't always doing this stuff. I used to work at a company. A pretty good one, too."

Komugi: "Seriously?"

Korogi: "Of course I worked seriously. That's what you have to do at a company."

Komugi: "So why did you—"

Kaoru snaps at them: "Hey, gimme a break, will ya? You're supposed to be talking about *this* stuff. You can yap about that shit somewhere else."

Komugi: "Sorry."

Kaoru reverses the video to 10:52 and sets it to play frame by frame, pausing it at one point and enlarging the man's image in stages. Then she prints the image, producing a fairly good-size color photograph of the man's face.

Komugi: "Fantastic!"

Korogi: "Wow! Look what you can do! Like *Blade Runner!*"

Komugi: "I guess it's handy, but the world's a pretty

scary place now if you stop and think about it. You can't just walk into a love ho any time you feel like it."

Kaoru: "So you guys better not do anything bad when you go out. You never know when there's a camera watching these days."

Komugi: "The walls have ears—and digital cameras."

Korogi: "Yeah, you gotta watch what you're doing."

Kaoru makes five prints in all. Each woman studies the man's face.

Kaoru: "The enlargement is grainy, but you can pretty much tell what he looks like, right?"

Komugi: "I'd definitely recognize him on the street."

Kaoru twists her neck, cracking and popping the bones, as she sits there, thinking. Finally, an idea comes to her: "Did either of you guys use this office phone after I went out?"

Both women shake their heads.

Komugi: "Not me."

Korogi: "Or me."

Kaoru: "Which means nobody dialed any numbers after the Chinese girl used the phone?"

Komugi: "Never touched it."

Korogi: "Not a finger."

Kaoru picks up the receiver, takes a breath, and hits the redial button.

After two rings, a man picks up the other phone and rattles off something in Chinese.

Kaoru says, "Hello, I'm calling from the Hotel Alphaville. You know: a guest of ours beat up one of your girls around eleven o'clock? Well, we've got the guy's photo.

From the security camera. I thought you might want one."

A few moments of silence follow. Then the man says in Japanese, "Wait a minute."

"I'll wait," says Kaoru. "Till I turn blue."

Some kind of discussion goes on at the other end. Ear on the receiver, Kaoru twiddles a ballpoint pen between her fingers. Komugi belts out a song using the tip of her broomstick as her mike: "The snow is fa-a-a-a-lling . . . But where are yo-o-o-o-o-u? . . . I'll go on wa-a-a-a-iting . . . Till I turn blu-u-u-u-e . . ."

The man comes back to the telephone. "You got the picture there now?"

"Hot off the press," says Kaoru.

"How'd you get this number?"

"They put all kinds of convenient features into these modern gizmos."

A few more seconds of silence follow. The man says, "I'll be there in ten minutes."

"I'll be at the front door."

The connection is cut. Kaoru frowns and hangs up. Again she pops the bones in her thick neck. The room falls silent.

Komugi speaks hesitantly. "Umm . . . Kaoru?"

"What?"

"Are you really gonna give those guys the picture?"

"You heard what I said before: I'm not gonna let that bastard get away with beating up an innocent girl. And it pisses me off he skipped out on his hotel bill. Plus, look at this pasty-faced salaryman son-of-a-bitch: I can't stand him."

Komugi: "Yeah, but if they find him, they might hang a rock on him and toss him into Tokyo Bay. If you got mixed up in something like that, there'd be hell to pay."

Kaoru is still frowning. "Nah, they're not gonna kill him. The police don't give a shit when those Chinese guys kill each other, but it's a different story when they start bumping off respectable Japanese. That's when the trouble starts. Nah, they'll just grab him and teach him a lesson, and maybe cut off an ear."

Komugi: "Ow!"

Korogi: "Kinda like van Gogh."

Komugi: "But really, Kaoru, d'you think they can find the guy with just a photo to go on? I mean, it's a big town!"

Kaoru: "Yeah, but once those guys make up their minds, they never let go. That's the way they are with stuff like this. If some guy off the street gets away with making them look bad, they can't keep their women in line, and they lose face with the other gangs. They can't survive in that world if they lose face."

Kaoru takes a cigarette from the desktop, puts it in her mouth, and lights it with a match. Pursing her lips, she slowly releases a long stream of smoke at the computer screen.

On the paused screen the enlarged face of the man.

*T*en minutes later. Kaoru and Komugi wait near the hotel's front door. Kaoru wears the same leather jacket as before, her woolen hat pulled down almost to her eyes. Komugi wears a big, thick sweater. She clutches herself across the chest to ward off the cold. Soon, the man who came to pick up the woman arrives on his big motorcycle.

He stops the bike a few paces away from the women. Again he keeps the engine running. He takes off his helmet, rests it on the gas tank, and deliberately removes his right glove. He stuffs the glove into his jacket pocket and stands his ground. He is obviously not going to move. Kaoru strides toward him and holds out three copies of the photo.

"He probably works in a company near here," she says. "I think he works nights a lot, and I'm pretty sure he's ordered women here before. Maybe he's one of your regulars."

The man takes the photos and stares at them for a few seconds. They don't seem to interest him especially.

"So?" he asks, looking at Kaoru.

"Whaddya mean, 'So?' "

"Why are you giving me these?"

"I kinda figured you'd wanna have 'em. You don't?"

Instead of replying, the man unzips his jacket and puts the photos, folded in half, into a kind of document sack hanging across his chest. Then he raises the zipper to the base of his neck. He keeps his eyes fixed on Kaoru the whole time.

The man is trying to find out what Kaoru wants in return for supplying him with this information, but he refuses to ask the question. He holds his pose, mouth shut, and waits for the answer to come to him. But Kaoru faces him with arms folded like his, aiming her cold stare at him. She is not going to back down, either. This suffocating stare-down goes on for some time. Finally Kaoru breaks the silence with a well-timed clearing of her throat.

"Just let me know if you find him, okay?"

The man grips the handlebar with his left hand and rests his right hand lightly on his helmet.

"Just let you know if we find him," he echoes mechanically.

"That's right."

"Just let you know?"

Kaoru nods. "Just a little whisper in my ear. I don't need to know what you do to him."

The man is thinking hard. He gives the crown of his helmet two light taps with his fist. "If we find him, I'll let you know."

"I look forward to the news," Kaoru says. "Do you guys still cut ears off?"

The man's lips twitched slightly. "A man has only one life. Ears, he has two."

"Maybe so, but if he loses an ear, he's got nothing to hang his glasses on."

"Most inconvenient," the man says.

This brings their conversation to an end. The man puts his helmet on, gives his pedal a big kick, turns the bike, and speeds off.

Kaoru and Komugi silently watch the motorcycle go, standing in the street long after it has disappeared.

When she speaks finally, Komugi says, "I don't know, he's kind of like a ghost."

"Well, it *is* the right time of day for ghosts, you know," Kaoru says.

"Scary."

"Yeah, really."

The two walk into the hotel.

. . .

*K*aoru is alone in the office. Her feet are on the desk. She picks up the photo and studies it again. Close-up of the man. Kaoru lets out a quiet moan and raises her eyes toward the ceiling.

7

O a.m.

A man is working at a computer. This is the man who was photographed by the surveillance camera at the Hotel Alphaville—the man in the light gray trench coat who took the key to room 404. He is a touch typist of awesome speed. Still, his fingers can barely keep up with his thoughts. His lips are tightly pursed. His face remains expressionless, neither breaking into a smile of satisfaction nor frowning with disappointment at the results of his work. The cuffs of his white shirt are rolled up to the elbows. His collar button is open, his tie loosened. Now and then he has to stop typing to scribble notes and symbols on a scratch pad next to the keyboard. He uses a long, silver-colored eraser pencil stamped with the company name: VERITECH. Six more of these silver pencils are neatly lined up in a nearby tray. All are of roughly the same length and sharpened to perfection.

The room is a large one. The man has stayed late to work in the office after everyone else has gone home. A Bach piano piece flows at moderate volume from a compact CD player on his desk. Ivo Pogorelich performs one of the English Suites. The room is dark. Only the area around the man's desk receives illumination from fluorescent lights on the ceiling. This could be an Edward Hopper painting titled *Loneliness*. Not that the man himself feels lonely where he is at the moment: he prefers it this way. With no one else around, he can concentrate. He can listen to his favorite music and get a lot of work done. He doesn't hate his job. As long as he is able to concentrate on his work, he doesn't have to be distracted by practical trivia. Unconcerned about the time and effort involved, he can handle all difficulties logically, analytically. He follows the flow of the music half-consciously, staring at the computer screen, moving his fingers at full speed, keeping pace with Pogorelich. There is no wasted motion, just the meticulous eighteenth-century music, the man, and the technical problems he has been given to solve.

His only source of distraction is an apparent pain in his right hand. Now and then he interrupts his work to open and close the hand and flex the wrist. The left hand massages the back of the right hand. He takes a deep breath and glances at his watch. He grimaces ever so slightly. The pain in his right hand is slowing his work.

The man is impeccably dressed. He has exercised a good deal of care in choosing his outfit, though it is neither highly individualized nor especially sophisticated. He does have good taste. His shirt and necktie look expensive—probably name-brand items. His face gives an impression of intelligence and breeding. The watch on his left wrist is elegantly thin, his glasses Armani in style. His hands are large, fingers long, nails well manicured. A narrow wedding band adorns the third finger of his left hand. His facial features are undistinguished, but the details of his expression suggest a strong-willed personality. He is probably just about forty years old, and the flesh of his face and neck, at least, show no trace of sagging. In general appearance, he gives the same impression as a well-ordered room. He does not look like the kind of man who would buy a Chinese prostitute in a love hotel—and certainly not one who would administer an unmerciful pounding to such a woman, strip her clothes off, and take them away. In fact, however, that is exactly what he did—what he *had* to do.

The phone rings, but he doesn't pick up the receiver. Never changing his expression, he goes on working at the same speed. He lets the phone ring, his line of vision unwavering. After four rings, the answering machine takes over.

"Shirakawa here. Sorry, but I am unable to take your call. Please leave a message after the beep."

The signal sounds.

"Hello?" says a woman's voice. It is low and muffled and sleepy-sounding. "It's me. Are you there? Pick up, will you?"

Still staring at the computer screen, Shirakawa grabs a remote control and pauses the music before switching on the speakerphone.

"Hi, I'm here," he says.

"You weren't there when I called before. I thought maybe you'd be coming home early tonight," the woman says.

"Before? When was that?"

"After eleven. I left a message."

Shirakawa glances at the telephone. She is right: the red message lamp is blinking.

"Sorry, I didn't notice. I was concentrating on my work," Shirakawa says. "After eleven, huh? I went out for a snack. Then I stopped by Starbucks for a macchiato. You been up all this time?"

Shirakawa goes on tapping at the keyboard as he talks.

"I went back to sleep at eleven thirty, but I had a terrible dream and woke up a minute ago. You still weren't home, so . . . What was it today?"

Shirakawa doesn't understand her question. He stops typing and glances at the phone. The wrinkles at the corners of his eyes momentarily deepen.

"What was what?"

"Your midnight snack. What'd you eat?"

"Oh. Chinese. Same as always. Keeps me full."

"Was it good?"

"Not especially."

He returns his gaze to the computer screen and starts tapping the keys again.

"So, how's the work going?"

"Tough situation. Guy drove his ball into the rough. If somebody doesn't fix it before the sun comes up, our morning net meeting's not gonna happen."

"And that somebody is you again?"

"None other," Shirakawa says. "I don't see anybody else around here."

"Think you can fix it in time?"

"Of course. You're talking to a top-seeded pro here. I score at least par on my worst days. And if we can't have our meeting tomorrow morning, we might lose our last chance to buy out Microsoft."

"You're gonna buy out Microsoft?!"

"Just kidding," Shirakawa says. "Anyhow, I think it'll take me another hour. I'll call a cab and be home by four thirty, maybe."

"I'll probably be asleep by then. I've gotta get up at six and make the kids' lunches."

"And when you get up, I'll be sound asleep."

"And when you get up, I'll be eating lunch at the office."

"And when you get home, I'll be settling down to do serious work."

"Here we go again: never meeting."

"I should be getting back to a more reasonable schedule next week. One of the guys'll be coming back from a business trip, and the kinks in the new system should be ironed out."

"Really?"

"Probably," Shirakawa says.

"It may be my imagination, but I seem to recall you saying the exact same words a month ago."

"Yeah, I cut and pasted them in just now."

His wife sighs. "I hope it works out this time. I'd like to have a meal together once in a while, and maybe go to sleep at the same time."

"Yeah."

"Well, don't work too hard."

"Don't worry. I'll sink that last perfect putt, hear the crowd applaud, and come home."

"Okay, then . . ."

"Okay."

"Oh, wait a second."

"Huh?"

"I hate to ask a top-seeded pro to do something like this, but on the way home can you stop by a convenience store for a carton of milk? Takanashi low-fat if they've got it."

"No problem," he says. "Takanashi low-fat."

Shirakawa cuts the connection and checks his watch. He picks up the mug on his desk and takes a sip of cold coffee. The mug has an Intel Inside logo. He restarts the CD player and flexes his right hand in time to Bach. He takes a deep breath and sucks in a new lungful of air. Then he flicks a switch in his head and gets back to his interrupted work. Once again the single most important thing for him is how to get consistently from point A to point B over the shortest possible distance.

The interior of a convenience store. Cartons of Takanashi low-fat milk line the dairy case. Young jazz musician Takahashi softly whistles "Five Spot After Dark" as he inspects the contents of the case. He carries only a shopping basket. His hand reaches out, grasps a carton of milk, but he notices that it is low-fat, and he frowns. This could well be a fundamental moral problem for him, not just a question of the fat content of milk. He returns the low-fat to its place on the shelf and picks up a neighboring regular. He checks the expiration date and puts the carton into his basket.

Next he moves on to the fruit case and picks up an apple. This he inspects from several angles beneath the ceiling lights. It is not quite good enough. He puts it back and picks up another apple, subjecting it to the same kind of scrutiny. He repeats the process several times until he finds one that he can at least accept, if not be wholly satisfied with. Milk and apples seem to have a special significance for him. He heads for the checkout counter, but on the way he notices some vinyl-wrapped fish cakes and picks one up. After checking the expiration date printed on the corner of the bag, he puts it into his basket. He pays the cashier and, shoving the change into his pants pocket, leaves the store.

Sitting on a nearby guardrail, he carefully polishes the apple with his shirttail. The temperature must have dropped: his breath is faintly white in the night air. He gulps the milk down, almost all in a single breath, after which he munches on the apple. He chews each mouthful with care, thinking. It takes time for him to eat the whole apple this way. He wipes his mouth with a wrinkled handkerchief, puts the milk carton and apple core into a vinyl sack, and goes over to throw them away in a trash bin outside the store. The fish cake he puts into his coat pocket. After checking the time on his orange Swatch, he reaches both arms straight up in a big stretch.

When he is through with all this, he chooses a direction and begins walking.

8

Our viewpoint has returned to Eri Asai's room. A quick scan reveals nothing changed. The night has deepened with the passage of time, however, and the silence is one degree heavier.

No, something *has* changed. Greatly.

The change is immediately obvious. The bed is empty. Eri Asai is gone. The bedding is undisturbed, but it is not as if she woke up and left while we were away. The bed is so perfectly made, there is no sign she was sleeping in it until a few moments before. This is strange. What could have happened?

We look around.

The TV is still on. It displays the same room it was showing before. A large, unfurnished room. Ordinary fluorescent lights. Linoleum floor. The picture, however, has stabilized, almost to the point of unrecognizability. The static is gone, and instead of bleeding into each other, the images have clear, sharp outlines. The channel connection—wherever it might be tuned in to—is steady. Like the light of the full moon pouring down on an uninhabited grassland, the TV's bright screen illuminates the room. Everything in the room, without exception, is more or less under the influence of the magnetic force emitted by the television set.

The TV screen. The Man with No Face is still sitting in the chair. Brown suit, black shoes, white dust, glossy mask adhering to his face. His posture, too, is unchanged since we last saw him. Back straight, hands on knees, face angled slightly downward, he stares at something straight ahead of him. His eyes are hidden by the mask, but we can tell they are locked on something. What could he be staring at with such intensity? As if responding to our thoughts, the TV camera begins to move along his line of vision. At the point of focus stands a bed, a single bed made of unadorned wood, and in it sleeps Eri Asai.

We look at the empty bed in this room and at the bed on the TV screen. We compare them in detail. The conclusion is inescapable: they are the exact same bed. The covers are exactly the same. But one bed is on the TV screen and the other is in this room. And in the TV bed, Eri Asai lies asleep.

We suppose that the other one is the real bed. It was transported, with Eri, to the other side while we were looking elsewhere (over two hours have passed since we left this room). All we have here is a substitute that was left in place of the real bed—perhaps as a sign intended to fill the empty space that should be here.

In the bed in that other world, Eri continues sleeping soundly, as she did when she was in this room—just as beautifully, just as deeply. She is not aware that some hand has carried her (or perhaps we should say her body) into the TV screen. The blinding glare of the ceiling's

fluorescent lamps does not penetrate to the bottom of the
sea trench in which she sleeps.

The Man with No Face is watching over Eri with eyes
that are themselves hidden from view behind their
shroud. He aims hidden ears toward her with unwavering
attention. Both Eri and the Man with No Face intently
maintain their respective poses. Like animals hiding in
camouflage, they curtail their breathing, lower their body
temperature, maintain total silence, hold their muscles in
check, and block out their portals of awareness. We seem
to be looking at a picture that has been paused, which is
not in fact the case. This is a live image being sent to us in
real time. In both that room and this room, time is passing
at the same uniform rate. Both are immersed in the same
temporality. We know this from the occasional slow rising
and falling of the man's shoulders. Wherever the intention of each might lie, we are together being carried along
at the same speed down the same river of time.

9

Skylark interior. Fewer customers than before. The noisy student group is gone. Mari is sitting by the window, reading again. Her glasses are off. Her hat is on the table. Her bag and varsity jacket are on the next seat. The table holds a plate of little square sandwiches and a cup of herbal tea. The sandwiches are half gone.

Takahashi comes in. He is not carrying anything. He looks around, sees Mari, and heads straight for her table.

"Hey, how's it goin'?"

Mari looks up, registers that it is Takahashi, and gives him a little nod. She doesn't say anything.

"Okay if I join you?" he asks.

"Fine," she says, her voice neutral.

He sits down facing her. He takes off his coat and yanks up the sleeves of his sweater. The waitress comes and takes his order: coffee.

Takahashi looks at his watch. "Three a.m. This is the darkest part of the night—and the hardest part. You're not sleepy?"

"Not especially."

"I didn't sleep much last night. Had a tough report to write."

Mari doesn't say anything.

"Kaoru told me you'd probably be here."

Mari nods.

Takahashi says, "Sorry for putting you through that. The Chinese girl, I mean. I was practicing and Kaoru called me on my cell phone and asked me if I knew anybody who spoke Chinese. None of us could, of course, but then I thought of you. I told her she'd find this girl named Mari Asai in Denny's, and what you look like and that you're fluent in Chinese. I hope it wasn't too big a pain for you."

Mari rubs the marks her glasses left on her skin. "No, don't worry."

"Kaoru says you were a tremendous help. She was really grateful. I think she likes you."

Mari changes the subject. "You finished practicing?"

"Taking a break," Takahashi says. "I wanted to wake myself up with some hot coffee—and say thanks to you. I was worried about the interruption."

"What interruption?"

"I don't know," he says. "I figured it must have interrupted *something* you were doing."

"Do you enjoy performing music?" Mari asks.

"Yeah. It's the next-best thing to flying through the air."

"Oh? Have you flown through the air?"

Takahashi smiles. He holds the smile while inserting a pause. "Not all by myself, no," he says. "It's just a figure of speech."

"Are you planning to be a professional musician?"

He shakes his head. "I'm not that talented. I love to play, but I could never make a living at it. There's a big difference between playing well and playing really creatively. I think I'm pretty good on my instrument. People say they like my playing, and I enjoy hearing that, but that's as far as it goes. I'm gonna quit the band at the end of the month and basically cut my ties with music."

"What do you mean, 'playing really creatively'? Can you give me a concrete example?"

"Hmm, let's see . . . You send the music deep enough into your heart so that it makes your body undergo a kind of a physical shift, and simultaneously the listener's body also undergoes the same kind of physical shift. It's giving birth to that kind of shared state. Probably."

"Sounds hard."

"It *is* hard," Takahashi says. "That's why I'm getting off. I'm gonna change trains at the next station."

"You won't even touch your instrument anymore?"

He turns his hands palm-upward on the table. "Maybe not."

"Gonna take a job?"

Takahashi shakes his head again. "No, that I'm *not* going to do."

After a pause, Mari asks, "Then what *are* you going to do?"

"Study law seriously. Take the National Bar Exam."

Mari keeps silent, but her curiosity seems to have been piqued.

"It'll take a while, I suppose," he says. "Officially, I've been in pre-law all along, but the band is all I've ever thought about. I've been studying law like it was just another subject. Even if I change my attitude and start studying hard now, it won't be easy to catch up. Life's not that simple."

The waitress brings his coffee. Takahashi adds cream, clanks his spoon around in the cup, and drinks.

Then he says, "To tell you the truth, this is the first time in my life I've ever wanted to study something seriously. I've never had *bad* grades. They weren't especially good, but they weren't bad, either. I could always get the point of things where it really mattered, so I could always manage with the grades. I'm good at that. Which is why I got into a pretty good school, and if I keep up what I'm doing now, I can probably get a job at a pretty good company. So then I'll probably make a pretty good marriage and have a pretty good home . . . you see? But now I'm sick of the whole thing. All of a sudden."

"Why?"

"Why did I suddenly start thinking I wanted to study seriously?"

"Yeah."

Holding his coffee cup between his hands, Takahashi narrows his eyes and looks at her as if peeking into a room through a crack in a window. "Are you asking because you really want an answer?"

"Of course. Don't people usually ask questions because they want answers?"

"Logically, yes. But some people ask questions just to be polite."

"I don't know. Why would *I* have to ask *you* questions just to be polite?"

"Well, true." Takahashi thought about this a moment and returned his cup to his saucer with a dry clink. "Okay. Do you want the long version or the short version?"

"Medium."

"You got it. One medium-size answer coming up."

Takahashi took a moment to get his thoughts in order.

"I attended a few trials this year between April and June. In the Tokyo District Court in Kasumigaseki. It was an assignment for a seminar: to sit in on a number of trials and write a report. Uh . . . have you ever been to a trial?"

Mari shakes her head.

Takahashi says, "The court is like a cinema complex. They've got this big board near the entrance where they list all the trials and their starting times like a program guide, and you pick one that looks like it might be interesting to you and you go and sit there as an observer. Anybody can get in. You just can't bring in any cameras or tape recorders. Or food. And you're not allowed to talk. Plus the seats are cramped, and if you doze off the bailiff gets after you. But you can't complain: the admission is free."

Takahashi pauses before continuing.

"I mostly attended criminal trials—assault and bodily injury, arson, robbery, and murder. Bad guys who did bad things and got caught and put on trial and punished. Those are the easy ones to understand, right? With economically or ideologically motivated crimes, you have to know the background, and things can get complicated. It's hard to tell good from bad. All I wanted to do was write my paper, get a halfway decent grade, and that would be that. Like a grade-school kid's summer homework assignment: keep a morning-glory observation diary."

Takahashi breaks off talking at that point. His hands are on the table. He looks at his own palms.

"After I'd been to the court a few times, though, and observed a few cases, I started to become strangely interested in viewing the events that were being judged and the people who were involved in the events. Maybe I should say I found myself less and less able to see these as other people's problems. It was a very weird feeling. I mean, the ones on trial are not like me in any way: they're a different kind of human being. They live in a different world, they think different thoughts, and their actions are nothing like mine. Between the world they live in and the world I live in there's this thick, high wall. At least, that's how I saw it at first. I mean, there's no way I'm gonna commit those vicious crimes. I'm a pacifist, a good-natured guy, I've never laid a hand on anybody since I was a kid. Which is why I was able to view a trial from on high as a total spectator."

Takahashi raises his face and looks at Mari. Then he chooses his words carefully.

"As I sat in court, though, and listened to the testimonies of the witnesses and the speeches of the prosecutors and the arguments of the defense attorneys and the statements of the defendants, I became a lot less sure of myself. In other words, I started seeing it like this: that there really was no such thing as a wall separating their world from mine. Or if there was such a wall, it was probably a flimsy one made of papier-mâché. The second I leaned on it, I'd probably fall right through and end up on the other side. Or maybe it's that the other side has already managed to sneak its way inside of us, and we just haven't noticed. That's how I started to feel. It's hard to put into words."

Takahashi ran his finger around the perimeter of his coffee cup.

"So once I started having thoughts like this, everything began looking different to me. To my eyes, this system I was observing, this 'trial' thing itself, began to take on the appearance of some special, weird creature."

"Weird creature?"

"Like, say, an octopus. A giant octopus living way down deep at the bottom of the ocean. It has this tremendously powerful life force, a bunch of long, undulating legs, and it's heading somewhere, moving through the darkness of the ocean. I'm sitting there listening to these trials, and all I can see in my head is this *creature*. It takes on all kinds of different shapes—sometimes it's 'the nation,' and sometimes it's 'the law,' and sometimes it takes on shapes that are more difficult and dangerous than that. You can try cutting off its legs, but they just keep growing back. Nobody can kill it. It's too strong, and it lives too far down in the ocean. Nobody knows where its heart is. What I felt then was a deep terror. And a kind of hopelessness, a feeling that I could never run away from this thing, no matter how far I went. And this creature, this *thing* doesn't give a damn that I'm me or you're you. In its presence, all human beings lose their names and their faces. We all turn into signs, into numbers."

Mari's eyes are locked on his.

Takahashi takes a sip of his coffee. "Am I being a little too grim here?"

"Don't worry, I'm listening," Mari says.

Takahashi returns his cup to its saucer. "Two years ago, there was this case of arson and murder in Tachikawa. A guy killed an old couple with an axe, grabbed their bankbook, and set fire to their house to get rid of the evidence. It was a windy night, and four houses burned down. The guy was sentenced to death. In terms of current Japanese legal precedent, it was the obvious sentence for a case like that. Any time you murder two or more people, the death sentence is almost automatic. Hanging. And this guy was guilty of arson, too. Plus, he was a real bastard. He had been locked up any number of times, usually for something violent. His family had given up on him years ago. He was a drug addict, and every time they let him out of jail, he'd commit another crime. In this case, he didn't show an ounce of remorse. An appeal would have been rejected for sure. His lawyer, a public defender, knew from the start he was going to lose. So no one could be surprised when they came back with a death sentence, and in fact nobody *was* surprised. I sat there listening to the judge read the verdict, taking notes, and thinking how obvious it was. After the trial, I took the subway home from Kasumigaseki, sat down at my desk, and started putting my notes in order when all of a sudden I got this absolutely hopeless feeling. I don't know how to put it: it was like the whole world's electricity supply suffered a voltage drop. Everything got one step darker, one step colder. Little tremors started going through my body, and I couldn't stop shivering. Soon I even felt my eyes tearing up. Why should that be? I can't explain it. Why did *I* have to lose it like that just because that guy got the death penalty? I mean, he was a total scumbag, beyond any hope of redemption. Between him and me, there shouldn't have been anything in common, no link at all. And yet, I had this deep emotional upset. Why should that have been?"

His question remains just that—a question, hanging in the air between them for a good thirty seconds. Mari is waiting for him to go on with his story.

Takahashi continues: "What I want to say is probably something like this: any single human being, no matter what kind of a person he or she may be, is all caught up in the tentacles of this animal like a giant octopus, and is getting sucked into the darkness. You can put any kind of spin on it you like, but you end up with the same unbearable spectacle."

He stares at the space above the table and heaves a long sigh.

"Anyhow, that day was a turning point for me. After that I decided to study law seriously. I figured that's where I might find whatever I was looking for. Studying the law is not as much fun as making music, but what the hell, that's life. That's what it means to grow up."

Silence.

"And that's your medium-size answer?"

Takahashi nods. "Maybe it was a little long. I've never told this to anybody before, so I had trouble gauging the size . . . Uh, those little sandwiches you've got sitting on your plate: if you're not planning to eat them, mind if I have one?"

"All that's left are tuna fish."

"That's okay. I love tuna fish. You don't?"

"No, I do, but mercury builds up in your body if you eat tuna fish."

"Yeah?"

"If you've got mercury in your body, you can start having heart attacks in your forties. And you can start losing your hair."

Takahashi frowns. "So you can't have chicken, and you can't have tuna?"

Mari nods.

"And both just happen to be some of my favorite foods."

"Sorry."

"I like potato salad a lot, too. Don't tell me there's something wrong with potato salad . . . ?"

"No, I don't think so," Mari says. "Except, if you eat too much it'll make you fat."

"That's okay," Takahashi says. "I'm too skinny as it is."

Takahashi picks up a tuna sandwich and eats it with obvious pleasure.

"So anyhow, are you planning to stay a student until you pass the bar exam?" Mari asks.

"Yeah, I guess so. I'll just be scraping by for a while, I suppose, doing odd jobs."

Mari is thinking about something.

Takahashi asks her, "Have you ever seen *Love Story*? It's an old movie."

Mari shakes her head.

"They had it on TV the other day. It's pretty good. Ryan O'Neal is the only son of an old-money family, but in college he marries a girl from a poor Italian family and gets disowned. They even stop paying his tuition. The two manage to scrape by and keep up their studies until he graduates from Harvard Law School with honors and joins a big law firm."

Takahashi pauses to take a breath. Then he goes on:

"The way Ryan O'Neal does it, living in poverty can be kind of elegant—wearing a thick white sweater, throwing snowballs with Ali MacGraw, Francis Lai's sentimental music playing in the background. But something tells me I wouldn't fit the part. For me, poverty would be just plain poverty. I probably couldn't even get the snow to pile up for me like that."

Mari is still thinking about something.

Takahashi continues: "So after Ryan O'Neal has slaved away to become a lawyer, they never give the audience any idea what kind of work he does. All we know is he joins this top law firm and pulls in a salary that would make anybody envious. He lives in a fancy Manhattan high-rise with a doorman out front, joins a WASP sports club, and plays squash with his yuppie friends. That's all we know."

Takahashi drinks his water.

"So what happens after that?" Mari asks.

Takahashi looks upward, recalling the plot. "Happy ending. The two live happily ever after. Love conquers all. It's like: we used to be miserable, but now everything's great. They drive a shiny new Jaguar, he plays squash, and sometimes in winter they throw snowballs. Meanwhile, the father who disowned Ryan O'Neal comes down with diabetes, cirrhosis of the liver, and Ménière's disease and dies a lonely, miserable death."

"I don't get it. What's so good about a story like that?"

Takahashi cocks his head. "Hmm, what did I like about it? I can't remember. I had stuff to do, so I didn't watch the last part very closely . . . Hey, how about a walk? A little change of atmosphere? There's a tiny park down the street where the cats like to gather. We can feed them your leftover tuna-mercury sandwiches. I've got a fish cake, too. You like cats?"

Mari nods, puts her book in her bag, and stands up.

Takahashi and Mari walk down the street. They are not talking now. Takahashi is whistling. A black Honda motorcycle passes close to them, dropping its speed. It is the bike driven by the Chinese man who picked up the woman at Alphaville—the man with the ponytail. His full-face helmet is off now, and he scans his surroundings with great care. Between him and them, there is no point of contact. The deep rumble of the engine draws close to them and passes by.

Mari asks Takahashi, "How did you and Kaoru get to know each other?"

"I've been doing odd jobs at that hotel for the past six months or so. Alphaville. Dirty work—washing floors and stuff. Some computer stuff, too—installing software, fixing glitches. I even put in their security camera. Only women work there, so they're happy to get a man's help once in a while."

"How did you happen to start working there specifically?"

Takahashi has a moment of confusion. "Specifically?"

"I mean, *something* must have led you to start working there," Mari says. "I think Kaoru was being purposely vague about it . . ."

"That's kind of a tough one . . ."

Mari keeps silent.

"Oh, well," Takahashi says, as if resigning himself to the inevitable. "The truth is, I once took a girl there. As a customer, I mean. Afterwards, when it was time to go, I realized I didn't have enough money. The girl didn't, either. We had been drinking and really hadn't thought much about that part. All I could do was leave my student ID with them."

Mari offers no comment.

"The whole thing's kind of embarrassing," Takahashi says. "So I went the next day to pay the rest. Kaoru invited me to stay for a cup of tea, and we talked about this and that, at the end of which she told me to start part-time work there the next day. She practically forced me into it. The pay's not much good, but they feed me once in a while. And my band's practice space was something Kaoru found for us. She *looks* like a tough guy, but she's actually a very caring person. I still stop in for a visit now and then. And they still call me if a computer goes out of whack or something."

"What happened to the girl?"

"The one who went to the hotel with me?"

Mari nods.

"That was it for us," Takahashi says. "I haven't seen her since then. I'm sure she was disgusted with me. I really blew it. But anyhow, it's no big deal. I wasn't that crazy about her. We would have broken up sooner or later."

"Do you do that a lot—go to hotels with girls you're not particularly crazy about?"

"Hell no. I couldn't afford it, for one thing. That was the first time I ever went to a love hotel."

The two continue walking.

As if offering an excuse, Takahashi says, "And besides, it wasn't my idea. She was the one who suggested we go to a place like that. Really."

Mari says nothing.

"Well, anyhow, that would be another long story if I got started," says Takahashi. "All kinds of stuff led up to what happened . . ."

"You seem to have a lot of long stories . . ."

"Maybe I do," he says. "I wonder why that is."

Mari says, "Before, you told me you don't have any brothers or sisters."

"Right. I'm an only child."

"If you went to the same high school as Eri, your family must be here in Tokyo. Why aren't you living with them? It'd be a lot cheaper that way."

"That would be another long story," he says.

"You don't have a short version?"

"I do. A *really* short version. Wanna hear it?"

"Uh-huh," Mari says.

"My mother's not my biological mother."

"So you don't get along with her?"

"No, it's not that we don't get along. I'm just not the kind of guy who likes to stand up and rock the boat. But that doesn't mean I want to spend every day making chitchat and putting on a smiley face at the dinner table. Being alone has never been hard for me. Besides, I haven't got such a great relationship with my father."

"You don't like each other?"

"Well, let's just say our personalities are different. And our values."

"What does he do?"

"To tell you the truth, I don't really know," Takahashi says. "But I'm almost one hundred percent sure that it's nothing to be proud of. And besides—this is not something I go around telling people—he spent a few years in prison when I was a kid. He was an antisocial type—a criminal. That's another reason I don't want to live with my family. I start having doubts about my genes."

"And *that's* your really short version?" Mari asks in mock horror, smiling.

Takahashi looks at her and says, "That's the first time you've smiled all night."

10

0 a.m.

Eri Asai is still sleeping.

The Man with No Face, however, who was sitting beside her and watching her so intently, is gone. So is his chair. Without them, the room is starker, more deserted than before. The bed stands in the center of the room, and on it lies Eri. She looks like a person in a lifeboat floating in a calm sea, alone. We are observing the scene from our side—from Eri's actual room—through the TV screen. There seems to be a TV camera in the room on the other side capturing Eri's sleeping form and sending it here. The position and angle of the camera change at regular intervals, drawing slightly nearer or drawing slightly farther back each time.

Time goes by, but nothing happens. She doesn't move. She makes no sound. She floats face-up on an ocean of pure thought devoid of waves or current. And yet, we can't tear ourselves away from the image being sent. Why should that be? We don't know the reason. We sense, however, through a certain kind of intuition, that *something* is there. Something alive. It lurks beneath the surface of the water, expunging any sense of its presence. We keep our eyes trained on the motionless image, hoping to ascertain the position of this thing we cannot see.

Just now, it seemed there might have been a tiny movement at the corner of Eri Asai's mouth. No, we might not even be able to call it a movement. A tremor so microscopic we can't be sure we even saw it. It might have been just a flicker of the screen. A trick of the eyes. A visual hallucination aroused by our desire to see some kind of change. To ascertain the truth, we focus more intently on the screen.

As if sensing our will, the camera lens draws nearer to its subject. Eri's mouth appears in close-up. We hold our breath and stare at the screen, waiting patiently for whatever is to come next. A tremor of the lips again. A momentary spasm of the flesh. Yes, the same movement as before. Now there is no doubt. It was no optical illusion. Something is beginning to happen inside Eri Asai.

Gradually we begin to tire of passively observing the TV screen from this side. We want to check out the interior of that other room directly, with our own eyes. We want to see more closely the beginning of faint movement, the possible quickening of consciousness, that Eri is beginning to exhibit. We want to speculate upon its meaning based on something more concrete. And so we decide to transport ourselves to the other side of the screen.

It's not that difficult once we make up our mind. All we have to do is separate from the flesh, leave all substance behind, and allow ourselves to become a conceptual point of view devoid of mass. With that accomplished, we can pass through any wall, leap over any abyss. Which is exactly what we do. We let ourselves become a pure single point and pass through the TV screen separating the two worlds, moving from this side to the other. When we pass through the wall and leap the abyss, the world undergoes a great deformation, splits and crumbles, and is momentarily gone. Everything turns into fine, pure dust that scatters in all directions. And then the world is reconstructed. A new substance surrounds us. And all of this takes but the blink of an eye.

Now we are on the other side, in the room we saw on the screen. We survey our surroundings. It smells like a room that has not been cleaned for a long time. The window is shut tight, and the air doesn't move. It's chilly and smells faintly of mold. The silence is so deep it hurts our ears. No one is here, nor do we sense the presence of something lurking in here. If there was such a thing here before, it has long since departed. We are the only ones here now—we and Eri Asai.

Eri goes on sleeping in the single bed in the center of the room. We recognize the bed and bedclothes. We approach her and study her face as she sleeps, taking time to observe the details with great care. As mentioned before, all that we, as pure point of view, can accomplish is to observe—observe, gather data, and, if possible, judge. We are not allowed to touch her. Neither can we speak to her. Nor can we indicate our presence to her indirectly.

Before long there is movement in Eri's face again—a reflexive twitching of the flesh of one cheek, as if to chase away a tiny fly that has just alighted there. Then her right eyelid flutters minutely. Waves of thought are stirring. In a twilight corner of her consciousness, one tiny fragment and another tiny fragment call out wordlessly to each other, their spreading ripples intermingling. The process takes place before our eyes. A unit of thought begins to form this way. Then it links with another unit that has been made in another region, and the fundamental system of self-awareness takes shape. In other words, she is moving, step by step, toward wakefulness.

The pace of her awakening may be maddeningly slow, but it never moves backward. The system exhibits occasional disorientation, but it moves steadily forward, step by step. The intervals of time needed between one movement and the next gradually contract. Muscle movements at first are limited to the area of the face, but in time they spread to the rest of the body. At one point a shoulder rises gently, and a small white hand appears from beneath the quilt. The left hand. It awakens one step ahead of the right. In their new temporality, the fingers thaw and relax and begin to move awkwardly in search of something. Eventually they move atop the bedcover as small, independent creatures, coming to rest against the slender throat, as if Eri is groping uncertainly for the meaning of her own flesh.

Soon her eyelids open. But, stabbed by the light of the fluorescent lamps ranged on the ceiling, the eyes snap shut again. Her consciousness seems to resist awakening. What it wants to do is exclude the encroaching world of reality and go on sleeping without end in a soft, enigmatic darkness. By contrast, her bodily functions seek positive awakening. They long for fresh natural light. These two opposing forces clash within her, but the final victory belongs to the power source that indicates awakening. Again the eyelids open, slowly, hesitantly. But again the fluorescent glare is too much. She raises both hands and covers her eyes. She turns aside and rests a cheek against the pillow.

Time passes. For three minutes, four, Eri Asai lies in bed in that same position, eyes closed. Could she have gone to sleep again? No, she is giving her consciousness time to accustom itself to the waking world. Time plays an important role, as when a person has been moved into a room with vastly different atmospheric pressure and must allow the bodily functions to adjust. Her consciousness recognizes that unavoidable changes have begun, and it struggles to accept them. She feels slightly nauseated. Her stomach contracts, giving her the sensation that something is about to rise from it. She overcomes the feeling with several long breaths. And when, at last, the nausea has departed, several other unpleasant sensations come to take its place: numbness of the arms and legs, faint ringing of the ears, muscle pain. She has been sleeping in one position too long.

Again time passes.

Finally she raises herself in bed and, with unsteady gaze, examines her surroundings. The room is huge. No one else is there. *What is this place? What am I doing here?* Again and again she tries to trace her memory back, but it gives out each time like a short thread. All she can tell is that she has been sleeping in this place: she is in bed, wearing pajamas. *This is my bed, these are my pajamas. That much is certain. But this is* not *my place. My body is numb all over. If I was asleep here, it was for a very long time, and very deeply. But I have no idea how long it could have been.* Her temples begin to throb with the determined effort of thinking.

She wills herself out from under the covers, lowering her bare feet cautiously to the floor. She is wearing plain blue pajamas of glossy material. The air here is chilly. She strips the thin quilt from the bed and dons it as a cape. She tries to walk but is unable to move straight ahead. Her muscles cannot remember how to do it. But she pushes onward, one step at a time. The blank linoleum floor questions her with cold efficiency: Who are you? What are you doing here? But of course she is unable to answer.

She approaches a window and, resting her hands on the sill, strains to see outside. Beyond the glass, however, there is no scenery, only an uncolored space like a pure abstract idea. She rubs her eyes, takes a deep breath, and tries to look out again. Still there is nothing to see but empty space. She tries to open the window but it will not move. She tries all of the windows in order, but they refuse to move, as if they have been nailed shut. It occurs to her that this might be a ship. She seems to feel a gentle rocking. *I might be riding on a large ship, and the windows are sealed to keep the water from splashing in.* She listens for the sound of an engine or a hull cutting through the waves. But all that reaches her is the unbroken sound of silence.

She makes a complete circuit of the large room, taking time to feel the walls and turn switches on and off. None of the switches has any effect on the ceiling's fluorescent lamps—or on anything else: they do nothing. The room has two doors—utterly ordinary paneled doors. She tries turning the knob of one. It simply spins without engaging. She tries pushing and pulling, but the door will not budge. The other door is the same. Each of the doors and windows sends signals of rejection to her as if each is an independent creature.

She makes two fists and pounds on the door as hard as she can, hoping that someone will hear and open the door from the outside, but she is shocked at how little sound she is able to produce. She herself can hardly hear it. No one (assuming there is anyone out there) can possibly hear her knocking. All she does is hurt her hands. Inside her head, she feels something resembling dizziness. The rocking sensation in her body has increased.

We notice that the room resembles the office where Shirakawa was working late at night. It could well be the same room. Only, now it is perfectly vacant, stripped of all furniture, office equipment, and decoration. The fluorescent lights on the ceiling are all that is left. After every item was taken out, the last person locked the door behind him, and the room, its existence forgotten by the world, was plunged to the bottom of the sea. The silence and the moldy smell absorbed by the four surrounding walls indicate to her—and to us—the passage of that time.

She squats down, her back against the wall, eyes closed, as she waits for the dizziness and rocking to subside. Eventually she opens her eyes and picks something up that has fallen on the floor nearby. A pencil. With an eraser. Stamped with the name VERITECH, it is the same

kind of silver pencil that Shirakawa was using. The point
is blunt. She picks up the pencil and stares at it for a long
time. She has no memory of the name VERITECH. Could
it be the name of a company, or of some kind of product?
She can't be sure. She shakes her head slightly. Aside
from the pencil, she sees nothing that promises to give
her any information about this room.

She can't comprehend how she came to be in a place
like this all alone. She has never seen it before, and nothing about the place jogs her memory. *Who could have
carried me here, and for what purpose? Is it possible I
have died? Is this the afterlife?* She sits down on the edge
of the bed and examines the possibility that this is what
has happened to her. But she cannot believe that she is
dead. Nor should the afterlife be like this. If dying meant
being shut up alone inside a vacant room in an isolated
office building, it was too utterly lacking any hope of sal-
vation. *Could this be a dream then? No, it is too consistent
to be a dream, the details too concrete and vivid. I can
actually touch the things that are here.* She jabs the back
of her hand with the pencil tip to verify the pain. She licks
the eraser to verify the taste of rubber.

This is reality, she concludes. *For some reason, a different kind of reality has taken the place of my normal
reality. Wherever it might have been brought from, whoever might have carried me here, I have been left shut up
entirely alone in this strange, dusty, viewless room with
no exit. Could I have lost my mind and, as a result, been
sent to some kind of institution? No, that is not likely,
either. After all, who gets to bring her own bed along*

when she enters the hospital? And besides, this simply doesn't look like a hospital room. Neither does it look like a prison cell. It's just a big, empty room.

She returns to the bed and strokes the quilt. She gives the pillow a few light pats. They are just an ordinary quilt and an ordinary pillow. Not symbols, not concepts; one is a real quilt, and the other a real pillow. Neither gives her anything to go by. Eri runs her fingers over her face, touching every bit of skin. Through her pajama top, she lays her hands on her breasts. She verifies that she is her usual self: a beautiful face and well-shaped breasts. *I'm a lump of flesh, a commercial asset,* her rambling thoughts tell her. Suddenly she is far less sure that she is herself.

Her dizziness has faded, but the rocking sensation continues. She feels as if her footing has been swept out from under her. Her body's interior has lost all necessary weight and is becoming a cavern. Some kind of hand is deftly stripping away everything that has constituted her as Eri until now: the organs, the senses, the muscles, the memories. She knows she will end up as a mere convenient conduit used for the passage of external things. Her flesh creeps with the overwhelming sense of isolation this gives her. *I hate this!* she screams. *I don't want to be changed this way!* But her intended scream never emerges. All that leaves her throat in reality is a fading whimper.

Let me get to sleep again! she pleads. *If only I could fall sound asleep and wake up in my old reality!* This is the one way Eri can now imagine escaping from the room. It's probably worth a try. But she will not easily be granted such sleep. For one thing, she has only just awakened. And her sleep was too long and deep for that: so deep that she left her normal reality behind.

She lodges the silver pencil between her fingers and gives it a twirl, vaguely hoping this thing she found on the floor will evoke some kind of memory. But all her fingers feel is an endless longing of the heart. Half-consciously, she lets the pencil drop to the floor. She lies on the bed, wraps herself in the quilt, and closes her eyes.

She thinks: *No one knows I'm here. I'm sure of it. No one knows that I am in this place.*

W*e* know. But we are not qualified to become involved with her. We look down at her from above as she lies in bed. Gradually, as point of view, we begin to draw back. We break through the ceiling, moving steadily up and away from her. The higher we climb, the smaller grows our image of Eri Asai, until it is just a single point, and then it is gone. We increase our speed, moving backward through the stratosphere. The earth shrinks until it, too, finally disappears. Our point of view draws back through the vacuum of nothingness. The movement is beyond our control.

The next thing we know, we are back in Eri Asai's room. The bed is empty. We can see the TV screen. It shows nothing but a sandstorm of interference. Harsh static grates on our ears. We stare at the sandstorm for a while to no purpose.

The room grows darker by degrees until, in an instant, all light is lost. The sandstorm also fades. Total darkness arrives.

11

Mari and Takahashi are sitting next to each other on a park bench. The park is a small one on a narrow strip of land in the middle of the city. Set near an old public housing project, it has a playground in one corner with swings, seesaws, and a water fountain. Mercury lamps illuminate the area. Trees stretch their dark branches overhead, and below there are dense shrubberies. The trees have dropped a thick layer of dead leaves that hide much of the ground and crackle when stepped on. The park is deserted at this hour except for Mari and Takahashi. A late-autumn white moon hangs in the sky like a sharp blade. Mari has a white kitten on her knees. She is feeding it a sandwich she brought wrapped in tissue paper. The kitten is eating with gusto. Mari gently strokes its back. Several other cats watch from a short distance away.

"Back when I worked in Alphaville, I used to come here on my breaks to feed and pet the cats," says Takahashi. "There's no way I can keep a cat now, living alone in an apartment. I miss the feel of them sometimes."

"You had a cat when you were living at home?" Mari asks.

"Yeah, to make up for not having any brothers or sisters."

"You don't like dogs?"

"I *like* dogs. I had a bunch of them. But finally, cats are better. As a matter of personal preference."

"I've never had a cat," says Mari. "*Or* a dog. My sister was allergic to the fur. She couldn't stop sneezing."

"I see."

"From the time she was a kid, she had a ton of allergies—cedar pollen, ragweed, mackerel, shrimp, fresh paint, all kinds of things."

"Fresh paint?" Takahashi says with a scowl. "Never heard of that one."

"Well, she had it. She had strong reactions, too."

"Like . . . ?"

"Like, she'd get a rash, and she had trouble breathing. She'd get these bumps in her windpipe, and my parents would have to take her to the hospital."

"Every time she walked past fresh paint?"

"Well, not *every* time, but it happened a lot."

"Even a lot would be tough."

Mari goes on petting the cat in silence.

"And how about you?" Takahashi asks.

"You mean allergies?"

"Yeah."

"I don't have any to speak of," Mari says. "I've never been sick. In our house, we had the delicate Snow White and the hardy shepherd girl."

"One Snow White per family is plenty."

Mari nods.

"And there's nothing wrong with being a hardy shepherd girl. You don't have to worry how dry the paint is every time."

Mari looks him in the face. "It's not that simple, you know."

"I know," Takahashi says. "It's *not* that simple . . . Say, aren't you cold out here?"

"No, I'm fine."

Mari tears off another piece of tuna sandwich and feeds it to the kitten. The kitten hungrily gobbles it down.

Takahashi hesitates for a few moments, unsure if he should mention something, then he decides to go ahead. "You know, your sister and I once had a long, serious conversation, just the two of us."

Mari looks at him. "When was that?"

"I don't know, maybe April. I was going to Tower Records one evening to look for something when I bumped into her out front. I was alone, and so was she. We stood on the sidewalk making small talk, but after a while we realized we had too much to say, so we went to a café down the street. At first it was nothing much, just the usual stuff you talk about when you bump into an old classmate you haven't seen for a while—like, whatever happened to so-and-so and stuff. But then she suggested we go some place we could have a drink, and the conversation turned pretty deep and personal. She had a lot she wanted to talk about."

"Deep and personal?"

"Yeah."

Mari looks at him questioningly. "Why would Eri talk to *you* about stuff like that? I never got the sense that you and she were particularly close."

"No, obviously, we're not. That time we all went to the hotel pool together was the first time I ever really talked to her. I'm not even sure she knew my full name."

Mari goes on stroking the kitten in silence.

Takahashi continues, "But that day, she wanted *somebody* to talk with. Normally it would have been another girl, a good friend. But I don't know, maybe your sister doesn't have any girlfriends she can open up to like that. So she picked me instead. It just happened to be me. It could have been anybody."

"Still, why *you*? As far as I know, she's never had any trouble finding boyfriends."

"No, I'm sure you're right."

"But she happens to bump into *you* on the street, somebody she doesn't know all that well, and she gets involved in this deep, personal conversation. I wonder why?"

"I don't know," Takahashi says, giving it some thought. "Maybe I seemed harmless to her."

"Harmless?"

"Yeah, like she could let herself open up to me this one time and not feel threatened."

"I don't get it."

"Well, maybe it's . . ." Takahashi seems to be having trouble getting the words out. "This is gonna sound kinda weird, but people often think I'm gay. Like, on the street, sometimes some guy—a total stranger—will hit on me."

"But you're not gay, right?"

"No, I don't think so . . . It's just that people always seem to pick me to tell their secrets to. Guys, girls, people I hardly know, people I've never even met before: they open up to me about their wildest innermost secrets. I wonder why that is? It's not as if I *want* to hear this stuff."

Mari mentally chews over what he has just said to her. Then she says, "So, anyway, Eri confessed all these secrets to you."

"Right. Or maybe I should say she told me *personal* stuff."

"Like, for example . . . ?" Mari asks.

"Like, say, family stuff."

"Family stuff?"

"Just for example," Takahashi says.

"Including stuff about me?"

"Uh-huh."

"What kind of stuff?"

Takahashi takes a moment to think how best to say this. "For example, she said she wishes she could be closer to you."

"*Closer* to me?"

"She felt that you had deliberately put a kind of distance between the two of you. Ever since you reached a certain age."

Mari softly embraces the kitten between her palms. Her hands feel its tiny warmth.

"Yeah," Mari says. "But it's possible for people to draw closer to each other even while they keep a reasonable distance between them."

"Of course it's possible," Takahashi says. "But what seems like a reasonable distance to one person might feel too far to somebody else."

A big brown cat appears out of nowhere and rubs its head against Takahashi's leg. Takahashi bends over and strokes the cat. He takes the fish cake from his pocket, tears the package open, and gives half to the cat, who gobbles it down.

"So that's the *personal problem* that was bothering Eri?" Mari asks. "That she can't get close enough to her little sister?"

"That was *one* of her personal problems. There were others."

Mari stays silent.

Takahashi goes on, "While she was talking to me, Eri was popping every kind of pill you can imagine. Her Prada bag was stuffed with drugs, and while she was drinking her Bloody Mary she was munching 'em like nuts. I'm pretty sure they were legal drugs, but the *amount* was not normal."

"She's a total pill freak. Always has been. But she's been getting worse."

"Somebody should stop her."

Mari shakes her head. "Pills and fortune-telling and dieting: nobody can stop her when it comes to any of those things."

"I kind of hinted to her she maybe ought to see a specialist—a therapist or psychiatrist or something. But she had absolutely no intention of doing that as far as I could tell. I mean, she didn't even seem to realize she had anything going on inside of her. I really started getting worried about her. I'm sitting there thinking, What could have happened to Eri Asai?"

Mari frowns. "All you had to do was give her a call afterwards and ask Eri directly—if you were really that worried about her."

Takahashi gives a little sigh. "To get back to our first conversation tonight, supposing I was to call your house and Eri Asai answered, I wouldn't have any idea what to say to her."

"But the two of you had that long, tight conversation over drinks—that deep, personal talk."

"True, but it wasn't exactly a *conversation*. I hardly said a thing. She just kept talking and I chimed in now and then. And besides, realistically speaking, I don't think there's a lot that I can do for her—as long as I'm not involved with her on a deeper, more personal level, at least."

"And you don't want to get that involved . . ."

"I don't think I *can* get that involved," Takahashi says. He reaches out and scratches the cat behind the ears. "Maybe I'm not *qualified*."

"Or to put it more simply, you can't be all that *interested* in Eri?"

"Well, if you put it that way, Eri Asai is not all that *interested* in *me*. Like I said, she just needed somebody to talk to. From her point of view, I was nothing much more than a wall with human features that could respond to her now and then as necessary."

"Okay, all that aside, are you deeply interested in Eri or not? Assuming you had to answer just yes or no."

Takahashi rubs his hands together lightly, as if confused. It's a delicate question. He finds it difficult to answer.

"Yes, I think I am interested in Eri Asai. Your sister has a completely natural radiance. It's really special and it's something she was born with. For example, when the two of us were drinking and having this intimate conversation, everybody in the bar was staring at us like, 'What the hell is that gorgeous girl doing with such a nothing guy?' "

"Yeah, but—"

"Yeah, but?"

"Think about it," Mari says. "I asked you if you were *deeply* interested in Eri, but you answered, 'I think I am interested' in her. You dropped the 'deeply.' It seems to me you're leaving something out."

Takahashi is impressed with Mari. "You're very observant."

Mari awaits his answer in silence.

Takahashi is not quite sure how to respond. "But . . . let's see . . . I'm sitting there having this long talk with your sister and, like, I begin to get this, uh, weird feeling. At first I don't notice just how weird it is, but the more time that goes by, the stronger it gets, like, I'm not even here: I'm not included in what's going on here. She's sitting right there in front of me, but at the same time she's a million miles away."

Still, Mari says nothing. Lightly biting her lip, she waits for the rest of the story. Takahashi takes his time searching for the right words.

"Finally, no matter what I say, it doesn't reach her. This *layer,* like some kind of transparent *sponge* kind of thing, stands there between Eri Asai and me, and the words that come out of my mouth have to pass through it, and when that happens, the sponge sucks almost all the nutrients right out of them. She's not listening to anything I say— not *really*. The longer we talk, the more clearly I can see what's happening. So then the words that come out of *her* mouth stop making it all the way to me. It was a very strange feeling."

Realizing that the tuna sandwiches are gone, the kitten twists itself out of Mari's hands and jumps down to the ground, running over to the thick shrubbery and all but leaping in. Mari crumples the tissue in which the sandwiches were wrapped and stuffs it into her bag. She rubs the bread crumbs from her hands.

Takahashi looks at Mari. "Do you understand what I'm saying?"

"Do I understand?" Mari says and takes a breath. "What you just described is probably pretty close to something I've been feeling about Eri for a very long time—at least the past few years."

"Like your words don't reach her?"

"Yeah."

Takahashi throws the rest of his fish cake to another cat that is edging toward him. The cat sniffs it cautiously and then devours it excitedly.

"I've got one more question," says Mari. "But will you promise to give me an honest answer?"

"Sure," Takahashi says.

"The girl you took to the Alphaville wasn't by any chance my sister, was she?"

With a shocked expression, Takahashi raises his face and looks straight at Mari. He could be looking at ripples spreading on the surface of a small pond.

"What makes you think that?" Takahashi asks.

"I dunno, just a feeling. Am I wrong?"

"No, it wasn't Eri. It was another girl."

"Are you sure?"

"I'm sure."

Mari thinks about something for a moment.

"Can I ask you one more question?"

"Of course."

"Say you took my sister to that hotel and had sex with her. Hypothetically speaking."

"Hypothetically speaking."

"And if, hypothetically speaking, I were to ask you, 'Did you take my sister to that hotel and have sex with her?' "

"Hypothetically speaking."

"If I did that, do you think you would honestly answer yes?"

Takahashi thinks about this for a moment.

"Probably not," he says. "I'd probably answer no."

"Why?"

" 'Cause it would compromise your sister's privacy."

"Kinda like professional confidentiality?"

"Kinda, yeah."

"Well, in that case, wouldn't the right answer be 'I can't answer that'? If you really have to keep things confidential."

Takahashi says, "Yeah, but if I were to say 'I can't answer that' in this context, it'd be like a de facto yes. That's willful negligence."

"So in either case, the answer would have to be no, wouldn't it?"

"Theoretically, yes."

Mari looks straight into Takahashi's eyes. "To tell you the truth, it doesn't matter to me either way, even if you slept with Eri—as long as it was something she wanted."

"Maybe not even Eri Asai has a clear grasp of what Eri

Asai wants. Anyhow, let's stop this. Both theoretically and in reality, the girl I took to Alphaville was somebody else, not Eri Asai."

Mari releases a little sigh and allows a few seconds to elapse.

"I do wish I could have been closer to Eri," she says. "I felt it especially in my early teens—that I wanted to be best friends with her. Of course, I idolized her to some extent: that was part of it. But she was already insanely busy even then—modeling for the covers of girls' magazines, taking a million lessons, everybody waiting on her hand and foot. She just didn't have any openings for me. In other words, when I needed her most, she had the least freedom to respond to my need."

Takahashi listens to Mari in silence.

"We were sisters living under the same roof, but we grew up in two different worlds. We didn't even eat the same food. With all those allergies of hers, she had to have a special diet that was different from what the rest of us ate."

Pause.

Mari says, "I'm not blaming her for anything. It's true at the time I thought my mother was spoiling her, but I don't care about that now. All I'm trying to say is that we've got this . . . *history* between us. So when I hear now that she wishes we could have been closer, I honestly have absolutely no idea what to do about it. Do you understand my feeling?"

"I think I do."

Mari says nothing.

"It suddenly popped into my mind when I was talking

with Eri Asai," Takahashi says, "but I think she's always had some kind of complex where you're concerned—from way back."

"Complex?" says Mari. "Eri toward me?"

"Uh-huh."

"And not the other way around?"

"No, not the other way around."

"What makes you think that?"

"Well, look. You're the kid sister, but you always had a good, clear image of what you wanted for yourself. You were able to say no when you had to, and you did things at your own pace. But Eri Asai couldn't do that. From the time she was a little girl, her job was to play her assigned role and satisfy the people around her. She worked hard to be a perfect little Snow White—if I can borrow your name for her. It's true that everybody made a big fuss over her, but I'll bet that was really tough for her sometimes. At one of the most crucial points in her life, she didn't have a chance to establish a firm self. If 'complex' is too strong a word, let's just say she probably envied you."

"Did Eri tell you that?"

"No, I just picked up on stuff around the margins of what she said, and put it together just now in my imagination. I think I'm not too far off."

"Maybe not, but I think you're exaggerating," Mari says. "It may be true that I've lived a more autonomous lifestyle than Eri. I understand that. But look at the actual results: here I am, insignificant and practically powerless. I don't have the knowledge I should have, and I'm not all that smart. I'm not pretty, and nobody's much concerned about me. Talk about establishing a firm self: I don't see where I've managed to do that, either. I'm just stumbling around all the time in my own narrow little world. What is there about me for Eri to envy?"

"This is still kind of a preparatory stage for you," Takahashi says. "It's too soon to reach any conclusions. You're probably a late bloomer."

"That girl was nineteen, too," Mari says.

"What girl?"

"The Chinese girl in Alphaville—all beat up and stripped naked and bloody. She was pretty. But there aren't any preparatory stages in the world she lives in. Nobody stops to think about whether she's a late bloomer or not. See what I mean?"

Takahashi offers his wordless affirmation.

Mari says, "The minute I saw her, I felt—really strongly—that I wanted to be her friend. And if we had met in a different place at a different time, I'm sure we could have been good friends. I've hardly ever felt that way about anybody. Hardly ever? Never would be more like it."

"Hmmm."

"But it doesn't matter how I feel: the worlds we live in are too different. And there's nothing I can do about it. No matter how hard I try."

"True."

"I can tell you this, though: I didn't spend much time with her, and we hardly talked at all, but I feel as if she's living inside me now. Like she's part of me. I don't know how to put it."

"You can feel her pain."

"Maybe so."

Takahashi broods over something for a while. Then he opens his mouth and says, "I just had an idea. Why don't you look at it this way? Say your sister is in some other Alphaville kind of place—I don't know where—and somebody is subjecting her to meaningless violence. She's raising wordless screams and bleeding invisible blood."

"In a metaphorical sense?"

"Probably," Takahashi says.

"Talking with Eri gave you this impression?"

"She's carrying around so many problems all by herself she can't make any headway, and she's searching for help. She expresses those feelings by hurting herself. This is not just an impression: it's clearer than that."

Mari stands up from the bench and looks at the sky. Then she goes over to the swings and sits in one. The night is momentarily filled with the crackling of the dry leaves under her yellow sneakers. She touches the swing's thick ropes as if to gauge their strength. Takahashi also leaves the bench and walks across the dried leaves to sit in the swing next to Mari's.

"Eri's asleep now," Mari says, as if sharing a confession. "She's in a really deep sleep."

"Everybody's asleep now," Takahashi says. "It's the middle of the night."

"No, that's not what I mean," Mari says. "She doesn't want to wake up."

a.m.

12

Shirakawa's office.

Naked from the waist up, Shirakawa is lying on the floor, doing sit-ups on a yoga mat. His shirt and tie hang on the back of his chair, his glasses and watch are lined up on his desk. Shirakawa has a slender build, but he is thick in the chest, and his midsection has no excess flesh. His muscles are hard and well defined. He makes a very different impression when undressed. His breaths are deep but sharp as he quickly raises himself from the mat and twists his torso right and left. Fine beads of sweat on his chest and shoulders shine in the light of the fluorescent lamps. A Scarlatti cantata sung by Brian Asawa flows from the portable CD player on the desk. Its leisurely tempo feels mismatched to the strenuousness of the exercise, but Shirakawa is subtly controlling his movements in time with the music. This all seems to be part of a daily routine whereby he prepares for his trip home after a night's work by performing a lonely series of exercises on the office floor while listening to classical music. His movements are systematic and confident.

After a set number of deep knee bends, he rolls up the

yoga mat and stores it in a locker. He takes a small white towel and a vinyl shaving kit from a shelf and brings them to the lavatory. Still naked from the waist up, he washes his face and dries it with the towel, which he then uses to wipe the sweat from his body. He performs each movement deliberately. He has left the lavatory door open and can hear the Scarlatti playing. He hums occasional passages of this music created in the seventeenth century. He takes a small bottle of deodorant from his shaving kit and gives each armpit a quick spray, then ducks his head to check for odor. He opens and closes his right hand several times and experiments with moving his fingers a few different ways. He checks the back of the hand for swelling. It is not bad enough to be noticeable, but he still feels a good deal of pain from it.

He takes a small brush from the bag and puts his hair in order. The hairline has retreated somewhat, but the well-shaped forehead gives no impression that anything has been lost. He puts his glasses on. He buttons his shirt and ties his tie. Pale gray shirt, dark blue paisley tie. Watching himself in the mirror, he straightens the collar and smooths the dimple below the knot.

Shirakawa inspects his face in the mirror. The muscles of his face remain immobile as he stares at himself long and hard with severe eyes. His hands rest on the sink. He holds his breath and never blinks, fully expecting that, if he were to stay like this long enough, some *other thing* might emerge. To objectify all the senses, to flatten the consciousness, to put a temporary freeze on logic, to bring the advance of time to a halt if only momentarily— this is what he is trying to do: to fuse his being with the scene behind him, to make everything look like a neutral still life.

Try as he might to suppress his own presence, that *other thing* never emerges. His image in the mirror remains just that: an image of himself in reality. A reflection of what is there. He gives up, takes a deep breath, filling his lungs with new air, and straightens his posture. Relaxing his muscles, he rolls his head in two big circles. Then he picks up his personal articles from the sink and places them in the vinyl bag again. He balls up the towel he used to dry his body and throws it in the wastebasket. He turns the light out as he exits the lavatory. The door closes.

Even after Shirakawa has left, our point of view remains in the lavatory, and, as a stationary camera, continues to capture the dark mirror. Shirakawa's reflection is still there in the mirror. Shirakawa—or perhaps we should say his image—is looking in this direction from within the mirror. It does not move or change expression. It simply stares straight ahead. Eventually, however, as though giving up, it relaxes, takes a deep breath, and rolls its head. Then it brings its hand to its face and rubs its cheek a few times, as if checking for the touch of flesh.

At his desk, thinking, Shirakawa twirls a silver-colored pencil between his fingers. It is the same pencil as the one on the floor of the room in which Eri Asai woke up, stamped with the name VERITECH. The point is dull. After playing with this pencil for a while, Shirakawa puts it down beside the pencil tray containing six identical pencils. These other pencils are sharpened to perfection.

He prepares to go home. He stuffs papers into a brown briefcase and puts on his suitcoat. He returns his shaving kit to his locker, picks up a large shopping bag that he had set down nearby, and carries it to his desk. He sits down and begins taking one item after another from the bag, examining each in turn. These are the pieces of clothing he stripped from the Chinese prostitute at Alphaville.

A thin cream-colored coat and red pumps. The shoe bottoms are worn out of shape. A deep pink, beaded crew-neck sweater, an embroidered white blouse, a tight blue miniskirt. Black pantyhose. Underthings of an intense pink with unmistakably synthetic lace trim. These pieces of clothing give an impression that is less sexual than sad. The blouse and the undergarments are stained with black blood. A cheap watch. Black fake-leather purse.

All the time he inspects the items from the bag, Shirakawa wears an expression as if to say, "How did these things get here?" His look is one of puzzlement, with a hint of displeasure. Of course he remembers perfectly well what he did in a room at the Alphaville. Even if he tried to forget, the pain in his right hand would keep reminding him. Still, nothing here strikes his eye as having any valid meaning. It's all worthless garbage, stuff that has no business invading his life. He keeps the process going, however, impassively but carefully unearthing the shabby traces of the recent past.

He unfastens the clasp of the pocketbook and dumps its entire contents on his desk. Handkerchief, tissues, compact, lipstick, eyeliner, several smaller cosmetic items. Throat lozenges. Small jar of Vaseline, pack of condoms.

Two tampons. Small tear-gas canister for use against perverts on the subway. (Fortunately for Shirakawa, she didn't have time to take that out.) Cheap earrings. Band-Aids. Pill case containing several pills. Brown leather wallet. In the wallet are the three ten-thousand-yen bills he gave her at the beginning, a few thousand-yen bills, and some small change. Also a telephone card and a subway card. Beauty-salon discount coupon. Nothing that would reveal her identity. Shirakawa hesitates, then takes out his money and slips it into his pants pocket. *Anyhow, it's money I gave her. I'm just taking it back.*

Also in the bag is a small flip phone. The prepaid type. Untraceable. The in-phone answering machine is set to receive. He turns it on and presses the playback button. A few messages play, but all are in Chinese. Same male voice each time. Each sounds like an angry outburst. The messages themselves are short. Shirakawa cannot understand them, of course, but he listens to them all before switching off the answering machine.

He finds a paper garbage bag and throws everything but the cell phone inside, crushes the bundle down, and ties the mouth of the bag. This he puts into a vinyl garbage bag, presses out the air, and ties the mouth of that bag. The cell phone stays on his desk, separate from the other things. He picks it up, looks at it, and sets it down again. He seems to be thinking about what to do with it. It might have some use, but he hasn't reached a conclusion.

Shirakawa switches off the CD player, places it in the deep bottom drawer of his desk, and locks the drawer. After carefully cleaning the lenses of his eyeglasses with a handkerchief, he calls a cab, using the land line on his desk. He gives them his office address and name and asks them to pick him up at the service entrance in ten minutes. He takes his pale gray trench coat from the coat rack, puts it on, and stuffs the woman's cell phone into the pocket. He picks up the briefcase and the garbage bag. Standing at the door, he surveys the office and, satisfied that there are no problems, turns off the light. Even after all the fluorescent lamps go out, the room is not completely dark. The light from street lamps and billboards filters in through the blinds, faintly illuminating the room's interior. He closes the door and steps into the hallway. As he walks down the hall, hard footsteps resounding, he gives a long, deep yawn, as if to say, "So ends another day."

He takes the elevator down, opens the service door, steps outside, and locks it. His breath makes thick white clouds as he stands there waiting. Soon a taxi arrives. The middle-aged driver opens his window and asks if he is Mr. Shirakawa. His eyes flick down to the vinyl garbage bag Shirakawa is holding.

"It's not raw garbage," says Shirakawa. "It doesn't smell. And I'm going to throw it away near here."

"That's fine," the driver says. "Please." He opens the door.

Shirakawa gets into the cab.

The driver speaks to him in the rearview mirror. "If I'm not mistaken, sir, you've been in my cab before. I picked you up here just about this time. Let's see . . . your home is in Ekoda?"

"Close. Tetsugakudo."

"That's it, Tetsugakudo. Would you like to go there today, too?"

"Sure. Like it or not, it's the only home I've got."

"It's handy to have one place to go home to," the driver says, and steps on the gas. "But working this late all the time must be rough."

"It's the recession. All that goes up are my overtime hours, not my pay."

"Same with me," the driver says. "The less I take in, the longer I have to work to make up the difference. But still, sir, I think you've got it better. At least the company pays your cab fare when you work overtime. I mean it."

"Yeah, but if they're going to make me work this late, they're going to have to pay for my cabs. Otherwise, I couldn't get home," Shirakawa says with a sour smile.

Then he remembers. "Oh, I almost forgot. Can you go right at the next intersection and let me out at 7-Eleven? My wife wants me to do some shopping. It'll just take a second."

The driver says to the rearview mirror, "If we go right there, we're gonna have to get onto some one-way streets and make a detour. There are lots of other convenience stores along the way. How about going to one of those?"

"That's probably the only place that carries what she wants. And anyhow, I want to get rid of this garbage."

"Fine with me. It might run the meter up a little extra, though. Just thought I'd ask."

He turns right, goes partway down the block, and finds a place to park. Shirakawa gets out, holding the garbage bag, leaving his briefcase on the seat. The 7-Eleven has a mound of garbage bags out front. He adds his to the pile.

Mixed in with a lot of identical garbage bags, his bag loses its distinctiveness instantaneously. It will be collected with all the others when the garbage truck arrives in the morning. Without raw garbage inside, it is not likely to be torn open by crows. He glances one last time at the pile of bags and enters the store.

There are no customers inside. The young man at the register is involved in an intense conversation on his cell phone. A new song by the Southern All Stars is playing. Shirakawa goes straight to the dairy case and grabs a carton of Takanashi low-fat. He checks the expiration date. Fine. Then he takes a large plastic container of yogurt. Finally it occurs to him to pull the Chinese woman's cell phone from his coat pocket. He looks around to make sure no one is watching him and sets the phone down next to the boxes of cheese. The little silver telephone fits the spot strangely well. It looks as though it has always been sitting there. Having left Shirakawa's hand, it is now part of the 7-Eleven.

He pays at the register and hurries back to the taxi.

"Did you find what you wanted?" the driver asks.

"Sure did," Shirakawa answers.

"Good. Now we head straight for Tetsugakudo."

"I might doze off, so wake me when we get close, okay?" Shirakawa says. "There's a Showa Shell station along the way. I get off a little after that."

"Yes, sir. Have a nice snooze."

Shirakawa sets the vinyl bag with the milk and yogurt next to his briefcase, folds his arms, and closes his eyes. He probably won't manage to sleep, but he is in no mood to make small talk with the driver all the way home. Eyes closed, he tries to think of something that will not grate on his nerves. Something mundane, without deep meaning. Or possibly something purely abstract. But nothing comes to mind. In the vacuum, all he feels is the dull ache in his right hand. It throbs along with the beating of his heart, and echoes in his ears like the roar of the ocean. *Strange,* he thinks: *the ocean is nowhere near here.*

Having run for a while, the taxi with Shirakawa in it stops at a red light. This is a big intersection with a long red light. Also waiting for the light next to the taxi is the black Honda motorcycle with the Chinese man. They are less than a meter apart, but the man on the cycle looks straight ahead, never noticing Shirakawa. Shirakawa is sunk deep in his seat with his eyes closed. He is listening to the imaginary roar of the ocean far away. The light turns green, and the motorcycle shoots straight ahead. The taxi accelerates gently so as not to wake Shirakawa. Turning left, it leaves the neighborhood.

13

Mari and Takahashi sit in their swings in the deserted nighttime park. Takahashi is looking at her in profile. His expression says, "I don't understand." This is the continuation of their earlier conversation.

" 'She doesn't want to wake up?' "

Mari says nothing.

"What do you mean?" he asks.

Mari remains silent, looking at her feet, as if she cannot make up her mind. She is not ready for this conversation.

"Wanna walk a little?" Mari says.

"Sure, let's walk. Walking is good for you. Walk slowly; drink lots of water."

"What's *that* supposed to mean?"

"It's my motto for life. 'Walk slowly; drink lots of water.' "

Mari looks at him. Weird motto. She does not comment on it, however, or ask him about it. She gets out of the swing and starts walking. He follows her. They leave the park and head for a bright area.

"Going back to the Skylark now?" Takahashi asks.

Mari shakes her head. "I guess just sitting and reading in family restaurants is starting to bother me."

"I think I know what you mean," Takahashi says.

"I'd like to go back to the Alphaville if I can."

"I'll walk you over there. It's right near where we're practicing."

"Kaoru said I could go there any time I wanted, but I wonder if it's going to be a bother for her."

Takahashi shakes his head. "She's got a foul mouth, but she means what she says. If she told you to come over anytime, then it's okay to come over anytime. You can take her at her word."

"Okay."

"And besides, they've got nothing to do at this time of night. She'll be glad to have you visit."

"You're going back to do more practicing?"

Takahashi looks at his watch. "This is probably the last all-nighter for me. I'm gonna give it my best shot."

They return to the center of the neighborhood. Hardly anyone is walking along the street, given the time. Four in the morning: slack time in the city. All kinds of stuff is scattered on the street: aluminum beer cans, a trampled evening newspaper, a crushed cardboard box, plastic bottles, tobacco butts. Fragments of a car's tail lamp. Some kind of discount coupon. Vomit, too. A big, dirty cat is sniffing at a garbage bag, intent on securing a share for the cats before the rats can mess things up or dawn brings the ferocious flocks of crows. Over half the neon lights are out, making the lights of an all-night convenience store that much more conspicuous. Advertising circulars have been stuffed under the windshield wipers of cars parked along the street. An unbroken roar of huge trucks reverberates from the nearby arterial. This is the best time for the truckers to cover long distances, when the streets are empty. Mari has her Red Sox cap pulled down low. Her hands are thrust into the pockets of her varsity jacket. There is a stark difference in their heights as the two walk side by side.

"Why are you wearing a Red Sox cap?" Takahashi asks.

"Somebody gave it to me," she says.

"You're not a Red Sox fan?"

"I don't know a thing about baseball."

"I'm not much interested in baseball, either," he says. "I'm more of a soccer fan. So anyway, about your sister . . . we were talking before."

"Uh-huh."

"I didn't quite get it, but you were saying that Eri Asai wasn't going to wake up?"

Mari looks up at him and says, "Sorry, but I don't want to talk about that while we're walking along like this. It's kind of a delicate subject."

"I see."

"Talk about something else."

"Like what?"

"Anything. Talk about yourself."

"About myself?"

"Yeah. Tell me about yourself."

Takahashi thinks for a moment.

"I can't think of any sunny topics offhand."

"Okay, so tell me something dark."

"My mother died when I was seven," he says. "Breast cancer. They found it too late. She only lasted three months from when they found it till when she died. Just like that. It spread quickly; there was no time for a decent treatment. My father was in prison the whole time. Like I said before."

Mari looks up at Takahashi again.

"Your mother died of breast cancer when you were seven and your father was in prison?"

"Exactly."

"So you were all by yourself?"

"Right. He was arrested on fraud charges and got sentenced to two years. I think he was running a pyramid scheme or something. He couldn't get a suspended sentence because the damages were big and he had an arrest record from the time he was in a student-movement organization. They had suspected him of being a fundraiser for the organization, but he really had nothing to do with it. I remember my mother took me to visit him in prison once. It was freezing cold there. Six months after they locked him up, my mother's cancer was discovered, and she was hospitalized immediately. So I became a temporary orphan. Father in jail, mother in hospital."

"Who took care of you during that time?"

"I found out later my father's family put the money together for the hospital and my living expenses. My father had been cut off from his family for years, but they couldn't just leave a seven-year-old kid to fend for himself, so one of my aunts came to see me every other day, halfheartedly, and people in the neighborhood took turns looking after me—laundry, shopping, cooking. We lived in the old working-class area then, which was probably good for me. They still believe in 'neighborhood' over there. But for the most part, I think I was pretty much on my own. I'd make myself simple meals, get myself ready for school and stuff. My memories are pretty vague about that, though, like it all happened to somebody else, far away."

"When did your father come back?"

"I think maybe about three months after my mother died. Under the circumstances, they approved an early parole for him. Obviously, I was thrilled when my father came home. I wasn't an orphan anymore. Whatever else he might have been, he was a big, strong adult. I could relax now. He came back wearing an old tweed coat. I still remember the scratchy feeling of the material and the tobacco smell."

Takahashi pulls his hand from his pocket and strokes the back of his neck several times.

"But even though I was with my father again, I never felt really secure deep down. I don't know how to put it exactly, but things were never really *settled* inside me. I always had this feeling like, I don't know, like somebody was putting something over on me, like my real father had disappeared forever and, to fill the gap, some other guy was sent to me in his shape. Do you see what I'm saying?"

"Sort of."

Takahashi goes silent for a while before continuing his story.

"So anyway, this is how I felt back then: that my father should never have left me all alone like that, no matter what. He should never have made me an orphan in this world. No matter what the reason, he should never have gone to prison. Of course, at that age, I didn't quite know what a prison even *was*. I mean, I was seven years old. But I sort of got the idea that it was like some huge closet—dark and scary and sinister. My father should never have gone to a place like that."

Takahashi breaks off his story. Then he asks Mari, "Has your father ever gone to prison?"

She shakes her head. "I don't think so."

"Your mother?"

"I don't think so."

"You're lucky. You should be grateful that's never been a part of your life." Takahashi smiles. "I don't suppose you know that."

"Never thought about it."

"Most people don't. I do."

Mari glances at Takahashi.

"So, your father never went to prison after that?"

"No, he never had any more problems with the law. Or maybe he did. Come to think of it, he must have. He just wasn't the kind of guy who could walk the straight and narrow. But at least he never got involved in anything bad enough to send him back to prison. Once was probably enough for him. Or maybe, in his own way, he felt some degree of personal responsibility toward my dead mother and toward me. Anyhow, he became a respectable businessman—though it's true he operated in a kind of gray zone. He had some extreme ups and downs—filthy rich sometimes, barely scraping by at other times. It was like riding a roller coaster every day. Once he had a Mercedes-Benz with a chauffeur; another time he couldn't buy me a bicycle. We sneaked out of one house in the middle of the night. We never settled down in any one place, so I had to change schools every six months or so. Of course, I could never make any friends. It went on pretty much like this until I entered middle school."

Takahashi shoves his hands into his coat pockets again and shakes his head as if trying to thrust dark memories aside.

"Now, though, he's pretty much settled down. He's got that baby-boomer toughness. Like Mick Jagger being called 'Sir' now—it's *that* generation, just hangin' in there. He doesn't do a lot of soul searching, but he learns his lessons. I don't know what kind of work he's doing now. I don't ask and he doesn't tell. But he never misses a tuition payment. And sometimes, if the mood strikes him, he'll give me a little spending money. Certain things it's better not to know."

"Your father remarried, you said?"

"Yeah, four years after my mother died. He's not the shining-hero type who raises his kid all by himself."

"And he didn't have any kids with his new wife?"

"Nope, just me. Which is maybe why she raised me as if I was hers. I'm really grateful for that. So the problem is all mine."

"What problem?"

Takahashi smiles and looks at Mari. "Well, finally, once you become an orphan, you're an orphan till the day you die. I keep having the same dream. I'm seven years old and an orphan again. All alone, with no adults around to take care of me. It's evening, and the light is fading, and night is pressing in. It's always the same. In the dream I always go back to being seven years old. Software like that you can't exchange once it's contaminated."

Mari keeps silent.

"I try not to think about this stuff most of the time," Takahashi says. "It doesn't do any good to dwell on it. You just have to live one day at a time."

"Walk a lot; drink your water slowly."

"That's not it," he says. "Walk slowly; drink lots of water."

"One's as good as the other, I'd say."

Takahashi thinks this over seriously. "Hmm," he says. "You may be right."

This brings their conversation to an end. They walk on in silence. Puffing white breath, they climb the dark stairway and come out in front of the Hotel Alphaville. Its gaudy purple neon lights now seem fondly familiar to Mari.

Takahashi stops at the entrance and looks straight at Mari with an unusually somber expression.

"I have a confession to make," he says.

"What?"

"I'm thinking exactly the same thing you are. But today's no good. I'm not wearing clean underwear."

Mari shakes her head in disgust. "No more pointless jokes, please. They tire me out."

Takahashi laughs. "I'll come get you at six. If you like, we can have breakfast together. I know a restaurant nearby that makes a good omelet—hot and fluffy. Oh, do you think there's some problem with omelets as food? Like, genetic engineering or systematic cruelty to animals or political incorrectness?"

Mari thinks a moment. "I don't know about the political part, but if there's a problem with chickens, I suppose there must be a problem with eggs."

"Oh, no," Takahashi sighs, wrinkling his brow. "Everything I like seems to have a problem."

"I like omelets, too, though."

"Okay, then, let's find a point of compromise," Takahashi says. "I promise you—these are great omelets."

He gives her a wave and heads off toward the practice space. Mari resettles her cap and enters the hotel.

a.m.

14

Eri Asai's room.

The TV is switched on. Eri, in pajamas, is looking out from inside the screen. A lock of hair falls over her forehead. She shakes her head to sweep it away. She presses her hands against her side of the glass and begins speaking in this direction. It is as though a person had wandered into an empty fish tank at an aquarium and was trying to explain the predicament to a visitor through the thick glass. Her voice, however, does not reach our side. It cannot vibrate the air over here.

Something about Eri suggests that her senses are still numbed, as though she is unable to use the full force of her limbs. This is probably because her sleep was so very deep and long. She is trying, nevertheless, to gain some understanding, however limited, of the inscrutable circumstances in which she finds herself. Disoriented and confused though she may be, she is exerting all her strength to comprehend the logic underlying this place— the basis of its existence. Her emotional state communicates itself through the glass.

Which is not to suggest that she is shouting at the top

of her voice or making an impassioned appeal. She seems exhausted from having done precisely that. She knows all too well that her voice will not get through.

What she is trying to do now is to transform what her eyes grasp and her senses perceive into the simplest and most appropriate words she can find. And so the words themselves emerge directed half at us and half at herself. This is no simple task, of course. Her lips move only sluggishly and intermittently. It is as though she were speaking a foreign language: her sentences are all short, and irregular gaps form between her words. The gaps stretch out and dilute the meaning that ought to be there. We train our eyes intently upon her from our side of the glass, but we can not clearly distinguish between the words and the silences that Eri Asai is forming with her lips. Reality spills through her slim fingers like the sands of an hourglass. Thus time is by no means on her side.

Eventually she tires of directing her speech outward and closes her mouth in apparent resignation. A new silence comes to overlay the silence that is already there. With clenched fists, she begins knocking lightly on her side of the glass. She is willing to try anything, but the sound fails to reach this side.

It appears that Eri is able to see what is on this side of the TV's glass. We can guess this from the movement of her eyes. They seem to be shifting from item to item in her room (the room on this side): the desk, the bed, the bookcase. This room is where she belongs. She should be sleeping peacefully in the bed over here. But now it is impossible for her to pass through the transparent glass wall and return to this side. Some kind of agency or intent transported her to that other room and sealed her in there as she slept. Her pupils have taken on a lonely hue, like gray clouds reflected in a calm lake.

Unfortunately (we should say), there is nothing we can do for Eri Asai. Redundant though it may sound, we are sheer point of view. We cannot influence things in any way.

But—we wonder—who was that Man with No Face? What could he have done to Eri Asai? And where has he gone off to now?

Suddenly, before any answer can be given, the TV screen begins to lose its stability. The signal shudders. Eri Asai begins to blur and quiver slightly around the edges. Aware that something is happening to her body, she turns away and scans her surroundings. She looks up at the ceiling, down at the floor, and finally at her wavering hands. She stares at them as their edges lose their clarity. Her face looks apprehensive. What could possibly be happening? The harsh crackling sound of static rises. A strong wind seems to have picked up again on a distant hilltop somewhere. The contact point in the circuit connecting the two worlds is being shaken violently, threatening to obliterate the clear outlines of her existence. The meaning of her physical self is eroding.

"Run!" we shout to her. On impulse we forget the rule that requires us to maintain our neutrality. Our voice doesn't reach her, needless to say, but Eri perceives the danger on her own. She tries to escape. She heads away with rapid strides—probably toward a door. Her image disappears from the camera's field of view. The TV picture suddenly loses its earlier clarity, distorts, and all but disintegrates. The light of the picture tube gradually fades. It shrinks to a small, square window, and finally is extinguished altogether. All information gives way to nothingness, all sense of place is withdrawn, all meaning is dismantled, and the two worlds are divided, leaving behind a silence lacking all sensation.

A different clock in a different place. A round electric clock hanging on the wall. The hands point to 4:31. This is the kitchen of the Shirakawa house. Collar button open, necktie loosened, Shirakawa sits alone at the breakfast table, eating plain yogurt with a spoon. He scoops it directly from the plastic container to his mouth.

He is watching the small TV they keep in the kitchen. The remote control sits next to the yogurt container. The screen is showing pictures of the sea bottom. Weird deep-sea creatures. Ugly ones, beautiful ones. Predators, prey. Miniature research submarine outfitted with high-tech equipment. Powerful floodlights, precision arm. The program is called *Creatures of the Deep*. The sound is muted. His face expressionless, Shirakawa follows the movements on the screen while conveying spoonfuls of yogurt to his mouth. His mind, however, is thinking about other things. He is considering aspects of the interrelationship of thought and action. Is action merely the incidental product of thought, or is thought the consequential product of action? His eyes follow the TV image, but he is actually looking at something deep inside the screen— something miles beyond the screen.

He glances at the clock on the wall. The hands point to 4:33. The second hand glides its way around the dial. The world moves on continuously, without interruption. Thought and action continue to operate in concert. At least for now.

15

reatures of the Deep is still on the screen, but this is not the TV in the Shirakawa kitchen. The screen is far larger. The set is in a guest room at the Hotel Alphaville. Mari and Korogi are seated in front of it, watching with less than full attention. Each is in her own chair. Mari has her glasses on. Her varsity jacket and shoulder bag are on the floor. Korogi frowns as she watches *Creatures of the Deep,* but she soon loses interest and starts surfing channels with the remote control. None of the early-morning programming seems worth watching. She gives up and turns the set off.

"You must be tired," Korogi says. "Better lay down and get some sleep. Kaoru's having a nice nap in the back room."

"I'm not that sleepy," Mari says.

"Then how 'bout a nice hot cuppa tea?"

"If it's no trouble."

"Don't worry, tea's one thing we've got tons of."

Korogi makes green tea for two using tea bags and a thermos bottle.

Mari asks, "What time do you work to?"

"Me and Komugi are a team: we work from ten to ten. Straighten up after the overnight guests leave, and that's that. We do take naps now and then."

"Have you been at this job long?"

"Going on a year and a half, maybe. You don't usually stay at one place a long time in this line of work."

Mari pauses a moment, then asks, "Do you . . . mind if I ask a kind of personal question?"

"Ask all you want," Korogi says. "Might not be able to answer some things, though."

"You're not going to feel bad?"

"Nah, don't worry."

"You said you got rid of your real name?"

"That's right. I did say that."

"Why did you do that?"

Korogi lifts the tea bag from Mari's cup, drops it into an ashtray, and sets the cup in front of her.

" 'Cause it would've been dangerous for me to go on using it. For all kinds of reasons. Tell you the truth, I'm running away from . . . certain people."

Korogi takes a sip of her own tea. "You probably don't know this, but if you're seriously trying to run away from something, one of the best jobs you can take is helper at a love hotel. You can make a lot more money as a maid in a traditional Japanese inn—get lots of tips—but you have to meet people and talk to them. Working in a love hotel, you don't have to show your face to guests. You can work in secret, in the dark. They'll usually give you a place to sleep, too. And they don't ask you for CVs or guarantors 'n' stuff. You tell 'em you can't give 'em your real name, and they say, like, 'Okay, why don't we call you Cricket?'

'Cause they're always short of help. You got a lot of people with guilty consciences working in this world."

"Is that why people don't usually stay in one place for long?"

"That's it. You hang around in one spot too long and they find you sooner or later. So you keep changing places. There's love hotels everywhere, from Hokkaido to Okinawa, so you can always find work. I'm real comfortable here, though, and Kaoru's really nice, so I stayed on."

"Have you been running away a long time?"

"Hmm . . . going on three years now, maybe."

"Always taking jobs like this?"

"Yep. Here 'n' there."

"I suppose whoever or whatever you're running away from is pretty scary?"

"You bet. Really scary. But don't ask me any more about that. I try not to talk about it."

The two are quiet for a time. Mari drinks her tea while Korogi stares at the blank TV screen.

"What did you used to do?" Mari asks. "Before you started running, I mean."

"Back then, I was just another girl with an office job. Graduated from high school, went to work for a big trading company, nine to five, in a uniform. I was your age . . . around the time of the Kobe earthquake. Seems like a dream now. And then . . . something . . . happened. A little something. I didn't think too much about it at first. But then it dawned on me I was stuck: couldn't go forward, couldn't go back. I left everything behind: my job, my parents . . ."

Mari looks at Korogi, saying nothing.

"Uh, sorry, but what was your name again?" Korogi asks.

"Mari."

"Let me tell you something, Mari. The ground we stand on looks solid enough, but if something happens it can drop right out from under you. And once that happens, you've had it: things'll never be the same. All you can do is go on living alone down there in the darkness."

Korogi stops to think again about what she has just said and, as if in self-criticism, gently shakes her head.

"Of course, it could be just my own weakness as a human being—that events dragged me along because I was too weak to stop them. I should have realized what was going on at some point and woken up and put my foot down, but I couldn't. I don't have the right to be preaching to you . . ."

"What happens if they find you—I mean the ones that are chasing you?"

"Hmm . . . what happens, huh?" Korogi says. "Don't know, really. Rather not think about it too much."

Mari keeps silent. Korogi plays with the buttons on the TV remote control, but she doesn't turn the set on.

"When I finish work and get in bed, I always think: let me not wake up. Let me just go on sleeping. 'Cause then I wouldn't have to think about anything. I do have dreams, though. It's always the same dream. Somebody's chasing me. I keep running and running until they finally catch me and take me away. Then they stuff me inside a refrigerator kind of thing and close the lid. That's when I wake up, and everything I've got on is soaked with sweat. They're chasing me when I'm awake, and they're chasing me in my dreams when I'm asleep: I can never relax. The only time it lets up a little is here, when I'm enjoying small talk with Kaoru or Komugi over a cup of tea . . . You know, Mari, I've never told this to anyone before—not to Kaoru, not to Komugi."

"You mean that you're running away from something?"

"Uh-huh. I think they kinda suspect, though . . ."

The two fall silent for a while.

"Do you believe what I'm telling you?" Korogi asks.

"Sure, I believe you."

"Really?"

"Of course."

"I could be making it all up. You wouldn't know: we've never met before."

"You don't look like the kind of person who tells lies, Korogi," Mari says.

"I'm glad you said that," Korogi says. "I've got something to show you."

Korogi pulls her shirt up, exposing her back. Impressed in the skin on either side of her backbone is a mark of some kind. Each consists of three diagonal lines like a bird's footprint and appears to have been made there by a branding iron. The scar tissue pulls at the surrounding skin. These are the remnants of intense pain. Mari grimaces at the sight.

"This is just one thing they did to me," Korogi says. "They left their mark on me. I've got other ones, but in places I can't show you. *These* are no lie."

"How awful!"

"I've never shown them to anyone before. Just to you, Mari: I want you to believe me."

"I do believe you."

"I just had that feeling, like I could tell you, it would be okay. I don't know why."

Korogi lowers her shirt. Then, as if inserting an emotional punctuation mark, she heaves a great sigh.

"Korogi?" Mari says.

"Uh-huh?"

"Can I tell you something I've never told anybody before?"

"Sure. Go ahead," Korogi says.

"I've got a sister. My only sibling. She's two years older than me."

"Uh-huh."

"Just about two months ago, she said, 'I'm going to go to sleep for a while.' She made this announcement to the family at dinnertime. Nobody thought much about it. It was only seven p.m., but my sister always had irregular sleep habits, so it was nothing to be too shocked about. We said good-night to her. She had hardly touched her food, but she went to her room and got in bed. She's been sleeping ever since."

"Ever since?!"

"Yup," Mari says.

Korogi knits her brows. "She never wakes up?"

"She does sometimes, we think," Mari says. "The meals we leave on her desk disappear, and she seems to be going to the toilet. Every once in a while, she takes a shower and changes her pajamas. So she's getting up and doing the bare minimum needed to keep herself alive—but really, just the bare minimum. None of us has actually seen her awake, though. Whenever we look in, she's in the bed, sleeping—*really* sleeping, not just faking it. She seems practically dead: you can't hear her breathing, and she doesn't move a muscle. We shout at her and shake her, but she won't wake up."

"So . . . have you had a doctor look at her?"

"The family doctor comes to see her once in a while. He's just a general practitioner, so he can't run any major tests on her, but medically speaking, there doesn't seem to be anything wrong with her. Her temperature's normal. Her pulse and blood pressure are on the low side, but not enough to worry about. She's getting enough nourishment, so she doesn't need intravenous feeding. She's just sound asleep. Of course if this were a coma or something, that would be a huge problem, but as long as she can wake up once in a while and do what she has to do, there's no need for special care. We consulted a psychiatrist, too, but there's no precedent for symptoms like this. She announces 'I'm going to go to sleep for a while' and does exactly that: if she has such an inward need for sleep, he says, the best thing we can do is let her keep sleeping. Even if he was going to treat her, it would have to be after she woke up and he could interview her. So we're just letting her sleep."

"Don't you think you should have her tested at a hospital?"

"My parents are trying to take the most optimistic view—that my sister will sleep as much as she wants to, and one day she'll wake up like nothing ever happened, and everything'll go back to normal. They're clinging to that possibility. But I can't stand it. Or should I say, every once in a while I can't take it anymore—living under the same roof with my sister and not having any idea why she's out cold for two months."

"So you leave the house and wander around the streets at night?"

"I just can't sleep," Mari says. "When I try, all I can think of is my sister in the next room sleeping like that. When it gets bad, I can't stay in the house."

"Two months, huh? That's a long time."

Mari nods in agreement.

Korogi says, "I don't really know what's going on, of course, but it seems to me your sister must have some big problem she's trying to deal with, something she can't solve on her own. So all she wants to do is go to bed and sleep, to get away from the flesh-and-blood world for a while. I think I know how she feels. Or should I say, I know *exactly* how she feels."

"Do you have any brothers or sisters, Korogi?"

"Two brothers. Both younger."

"Are you close to them?"

"Used to be," Korogi says. "Don't know now. Haven't seen 'em for a long time."

"To be completely honest," Mari says, "I never knew my sister very well—like, how she was spending her days, or what she was thinking about, or who she was seeing. I don't even know if something was troubling her. I know this sounds cold, but even though we were living in the same house, she was busy with her stuff and I was busy with my stuff, and the two of us never really talked heart-to-heart. It's not that we didn't get along: we never had a fight after we grew up. It's just that we've been living very different lives for a long time."

Mari stares at the blank TV screen.

Korogi says, "Tell me about your sister. If you don't know what she's like inside, tell me just the surface things, what you know about her in general."

"She's a college student. Goes to one of the old missionary colleges for rich girls. She's twenty-one. Officially majoring in sociology, but I don't think she has any interest in the subject. She went to college because that's what she was expected to do, and she knows enough to pass her exams, that's all. Sometimes she'll throw a little money in my direction to write reports for her. Otherwise, she models for magazines and appears on TV now and then."

"TV? What program?"

"Nothing special. Like, she used to be the one showing the prizes to the camera on a quiz show, holding them up with a big smile. That show ended, so she's not on anymore. She was in a few commercials, too—one for a moving company. Stuff like that."

"She must be really pretty."

"That's what everybody says. She doesn't look the least bit like me."

"Sometimes I wish I had been born beautiful like that. I'd like to try it, just once, see what it's like," Korogi says with a short sigh.

Mari hesitates a moment, then says as if sharing a confession, "This may sound strange, but my sister really *is* beautiful when she sleeps. Maybe more beautiful than when she's awake. She's like transparent. I may be her sister, but my heart races just seeing her that way."

"Like Sleeping Beauty."

"Exactly."

"Somebody'll kiss her and wake her up," Korogi says.

"If all goes well," Mari says.

The two fall silent for a time. Korogi is still playing with the buttons on the remote control. An ambulance siren sounds in the distance.

"Tell me something, Mari—do you believe in reincarnation?"

Mari shakes her head. "No, I don't think so," she says.

"So you don't think there's a life to come?"

"I haven't thought much about it. But it seems to me there's no reason to believe in a life after this one."

"So once you're dead there's just nothing?"

"Basically."

"Well, I think there has to be something like reincarnation. Or maybe I should say I'm scared to think there isn't. I can't understand nothingness. I can't understand it and I can't imagine it."

"Nothingness means there's absolutely nothing, so maybe there's no need to understand it or imagine it."

"Yeah, but what if nothingness is not like that? What if it's the kind of thing that *demands* that you understand it or imagine it? I mean, *you* don't know what it's like to die, Mari. Maybe a person really has to die to understand what it's like."

"Well, yeah . . . ," says Mari.

"I get *so* scared when I start thinking about this stuff," Korogi says. "I can hardly breathe, and my whole body wants to shrink into a corner. It's so much easier to just believe in reincarnation. You might be reborn as something awful, but at least you can imagine what you'd look like—a horse, say, or a snail. And even if it was something bad, you might be luckier *next* time."

"Uh-huh . . . but it still seems more natural to me to think that once you're dead, there's nothing."

"I wonder if that's 'cause you've got such a strong personality."

"Me?!"

Korogi nods. "You seem to have a good, strong grip on yourself."

Mari shakes her head. "Not me," she says. "When I was little, I had no self-confidence at all. Everything scared me. Which is why I used to get bullied a lot. I was such an easy mark. The feelings I had back then are still here inside me. I have dreams like that all the time."

"Yeah, but I bet you worked hard over the years and overcame those feelings little by little—those bad memories."

"Little by little," Mari says, nodding. "I'm like that. A hard worker."

"You just keep at it all by yourself—like the village smithy?"

"Right."

"I think it's great that you can do that."

"Work hard?"

"That you're *able* to work hard."

"Even if I've got nothing else going for me?"

Korogi smiles without speaking.

Mari thinks about what Korogi said. "I *do* feel that I've managed to make something I could maybe call my own world . . . over time . . . little by little. And when I'm inside it, to some extent, I feel kind of relieved. But the very fact I felt I had to *make* such a world probably means that I'm a weak person, that I bruise easily, don't you think? And in the eyes of society at large, that world of mine is a puny little thing. It's like a cardboard house: a puff of wind might carry it off somewhere."

"Have you got a boyfriend?" Korogi asks.

Mari gives her head a little shake.

"Still a virgin?"

Mari blushes with a quick nod. "Uh-huh."

"That's okay, it's nothing to be ashamed of."

"I know."

"You just didn't happen to meet anybody you liked?" Korogi asks.

"There's one guy I used to see. But . . ."

"You didn't like him enough to go all the way."

"Right," Mari says. "I had plenty of curiosity, but I just never felt like doing that. I don't know . . ."

"That's fine," Korogi says. "There's no sense forcing yourself if you don't feel like it. Tell you the truth, I've had sex with lots of guys, but I think I did it mostly out of fear. I was scared not to have somebody putting his arms around me, so I could never say no. That's all. Nothing good ever came of sex like that. All it does is grind down the meaning of life a piece at a time. Do you see what I'm saying?"

"I think so."

"Someday you'll find the right person, Mari, and you'll learn to have a lot more confidence in yourself. That's what I think. So don't settle for anything less. In this world, there are things you can only do alone, and things you can only do with somebody else. It's important to combine the two in just the right amount."

Mari nods.

Korogi scratches her earlobe with her little finger. "It's too late for me, unfortunately."

"Let me just say this," Mari says with special gravity.

"Uh-huh?"

"I hope you do manage to get away from whoever's chasing you."

"Sometimes I feel as if I'm racing with my own shadow," Korogi says. "But that's one thing I'll never be able to outrun. Nobody can shake off their own shadow."

"Maybe that's not it," Mari says. After a moment's hesitation she adds, "Maybe it's not your own shadow. Maybe it's something else, something totally different."

Korogi thinks about that for a while, then gives Mari a nod. "I guess you're right. All I can do is try my best and see it through to the end."

Korogi glances at her watch, takes a big stretch, and stands up.

"Time to get to work," she says. "You should grab some shut-eye, and go home as soon as it gets light out, okay?"

"Okay."

"Everything's going to work out fine with your sister. I've got a feeling. Just a feeling."

"Thanks," Mari says.

"You may not feel that close to her now, but I'm sure there was a time when you did. Try to remember a moment when you felt totally in touch with her, without any gaps between you. You probably can't think of anything right this second, but if you try hard it'll come. She and you are family, after all—you've got a long history together. You must have at least one memory like that stored away somewhere."

"Okay, I'll try," Mari says.

"I think about the old days a lot. Especially after I started running all over the country like this. If I try hard to remember, all kinds of stuff comes back—really vivid memories. All of a sudden out of nowhere I can bring back things I haven't thought about for years. It's pretty interesting. Memory is so crazy! It's like we've got these drawers crammed with tons of useless stuff. Meanwhile, all the really important things we just keep forgetting, one after the other."

Korogi stands there holding the remote control.

"You know what I think?" she says. "That people's memories are maybe the fuel they burn to stay alive. Whether those memories have any actual importance or not, it doesn't matter as far as the maintenance of life is concerned. They're all just fuel. Advertising fillers in the newspaper, philosophy books, dirty pictures in a magazine, a bundle of ten-thousand-yen bills: when you feed 'em to the fire, they're all just paper. The fire isn't thinking, 'Oh, this is Kant,' or 'Oh, this is the *Yomiuri* evening edition,' or 'Nice tits,' while it burns. To the fire, they're nothing but scraps of paper. It's the exact same thing. Important memories, not-so-important memories, totally useless memories: there's no distinction—they're all just fuel."

Korogi nods to herself. Then she goes on:

"You know, I think if I didn't have that fuel, if I didn't have these memory drawers inside me, I would've snapped a long time ago. I would've curled up in a ditch somewhere and died. It's because I can pull the memories out of the drawers when I have to—the important ones and the useless ones—that I can go on living this nightmare of a life. I might *think* I can't take it anymore, that I can't go on anymore, but one way or another I get past that."

Still in her chair, Mari looks up at Korogi.

"So try hard, Mari. Try hard to remember all kinds of stuff about your sister. It'll be important fuel. For you, and probably for your sister, too."

Mari looks at Korogi without saying anything.

Korogi looks at her watch again. "Gotta go."

"Thanks for everything," Mari says.

Korogi waves and slips out.

Alone now, Mari scans the room anew. A little room in a love hotel. No window. The only thing behind the Venetian blind is a hollow where a window should be. The bed is hugely out of proportion to the room itself. The head of the bed has so many mysterious switches nearby, it looks like something from an airplane cockpit. A vending machine sells graphically shaped vibrators and colorful underthings cut in extreme styles. Mari has never seen such odd items before, but she is not offended by them. Alone in this offbeat room, she feels, if anything, protected. She notices that she is in a tranquil mood for the first time in quite a while. She sinks deeper into the chair and closes her eyes, and soon she is asleep. Her sleep is short but deep. This is what she has wanted for a long time.

16

The drab storage basement where the band is allowed to practice at night. No windows. High ceiling with exposed pipes. Smoking is prohibited here because of the poor ventilation. As the night draws to a close, the formal practice has ended and the musicians are jamming. There are ten of them altogether. Two are women: the pianist at the keyboard and the soprano-sax player, who is sitting this one out.

Backed up by electric piano, acoustic bass, and drums, Takahashi is playing a long trombone solo. Sonny Rollins's "Sonnymoon for Two," a midtempo blues. His performance is not bad, marked less by technique than by his almost conversational phrasing. Perhaps it is a reflection of his personality. Eyes closed, he immerses himself in the music. The tenor sax, alto sax, and trumpet throw in simple riffs every now and then. Those not playing are drinking coffee from a thermos jar, checking their sheet music, or working on their instruments as they listen. Some call out now and then to urge Takahashi on during the pauses in his solo.

Enclosed in bare walls, the music is loud; the drummer

plays almost entirely with brushes. A long plank and tubular chairs comprise a makeshift table, on top of which are
scattered takeout pizza boxes, the thermos jar of coffee,
paper cups, sheet music, a small tape recorder, and saxo-
phone reeds. The heating here is almost nonexistent.
People play in coats and jackets. Some band members sitting out have donned scarves and gloves. It is a bizarre
scene. Takahashi's long solo ends, the bass takes a chorus,
and the four horns join in for the final theme.

When the tune ends, they take a ten-minute break.
Everyone seems tired after the long night of practice, and
there is less chatting than usual. As they prepare for the
next tune, one musician stretches, another takes a hot
drink, another nibbles some kind of cookie, a couple go
out for a smoke. Only the pianist, a girl with long hair,
stays with her instrument during the break, trying out
new chord progressions. Takahashi sits in a tubular chair,
organizes his sheet music, dismantles his trombone, spills
the accumulated saliva on the floor, gives the instrument a
quick wipedown, and begins putting it into its case. He is
obviously not planning to participate in the next jam.

The tall young bass player comes over and taps him on
the shoulder. "That was a great solo, Takahashi. It had real
feeling."

"Thanks," he says.

The long-haired young man who was playing the trumpet asks him, "Are you calling it a night, Takahashi?"

"Yeah, I've got something to do," he says. "Sorry I can't
help with the clean-up."

a.m.

*T*he Shirakawa house kitchen. On the TV, a beep signals the hour and the NHK news begins. The announcer stares straight into the camera, dutifully reading the news. Shirakawa sits at the table in the dining area, watching the television at low volume. The sound is barely audible. Shirakawa has loosened his tie and is leaning back in his chair, his shirtsleeves rolled up to the elbows. The yogurt container is empty. He has no special desire to see the news. Nothing is likely to arouse his interest. He knows that. He just can't sleep.

On the table, he opens and closes his right hand slowly. This is no ordinary pain he is feeling: it is a pain with memories. He takes a green-labeled Perrier bottle from the refrigerator and uses it to cool the back of his hand. Then he twists off the cap, pours himself a glass of water, and drinks it. He takes off his glasses and massages himself intently around the eyes. Still he feels no sign of sleepiness. His body is clearly suffering from exhaustion, but something in his head is preventing him from sleeping. Something is bothering him, and he can't seem to get rid of it. He gives up, puts his glasses back on, and turns to the TV screen. The steel export dumping problem. Government measures to rectify the drastic rise of the yen. A mother who killed herself and her two children. She doused her car with gasoline and lit it. A shot of the blackened hulk of the car, still smoking. Time for the Christmas retail wars to begin.

The night is nearly over, but for him the night will not end so easily. Soon his family will be getting up. He wants to be asleep by then for sure.

a.m.

A room in the Hotel Alphaville. Mari is sunk deep in a chair, napping. Her feet, in white socks, rest on a low glass table. In sleep, she wears a look of relief. Her thick book lies facedown on the table, spread open at the halfway point. The ceiling lights are on. The brightness of the room is apparently of no concern to Mari. The TV is switched off and silent. The bed is made. The only sound is the monotonous hum of the heater on the ceiling.

a.m.

E ri Asai's room.

Eri Asai is back on *this* side now. She is sleeping in her own bed in her own room again. Face turned toward the ceiling, she lies utterly still. Even her breathing is inaudible. This is the same view we had the first time we entered this room. Heavy silence, sleep of frightening density. Waveless, mirrorlike surface of the waters of thought. She floats there face-up. We can find no hint of disorder in the room. The TV screen is cold and dead, like the far side of the moon again. Could she have succeeded in escaping from that enigmatic room? Could a door have opened for her somehow?

No one answers our questions. Our question marks are sucked, unresisting, into the final darkness and uncompromising silence of the night. All we know for sure is that Eri Asai has come back to her own bed in this room. As far as our eyes can tell, she has managed safely to return to this side, her outlines intact. She must have succeeded in escaping through a door at the last moment. Or perhaps she was able to discover a different exit.

In any case it appears that the strange sequence of events that occurred in this room during the night has ended once and for all. A cycle has been completed, all disturbances have been resolved, perplexities have been concealed, and things have returned to their original state. Around us, cause and effect join hands, and synthesis and division maintain their equilibrium. Everything, finally, unfolded in a place resembling a deep, inaccessible fissure. Such places open secret entries into darkness in the interval between midnight and the time the sky grows light. None of our principles have any effect there. No one can predict when or where such abysses will swallow people, or when or where they will spit them out.

Free of all confusion, Eri now sleeps decorously in her bed. Her black hair fans out on her pillow in elegant, wordless significance. We can sense the approach of dawn. The deepest darkness of the night has now passed.

But is this actually true?

a.m.

Inside the 7-Eleven. Trombone case hanging from his shoulder, Takahashi is choosing food with a deadly serious look in his eye. He will be going back to his apartment to sleep but will need something to eat when he wakes up. He is the only customer in the store. Shikao Suga's "Bomb Juice" is playing from the ceiling speakers. Takahashi picks up a tuna sandwich packed in plastic and a carton of milk. He compares the expiration date on this carton with those on other cartons. Milk is a food of great significance in his life. He cannot ignore the slightest detail where milk is concerned.

At this very instant, a cell phone on the cheese shelf begins to ring. This is the phone that Shirakawa left there shortly before. Takahashi scowls and stares at it suspiciously. Who could possibly have left a cell phone in a place like this? He glances toward the cash register, but there is no sign of the clerk. The phone keeps ringing. Takahashi finally takes the small silver phone in his hand and presses the talk button.

"Hello?"

"You'll never get away," a man's voice says instantly. "You will never get away. No matter how far you run, we're going to get you."

The voice is flat, as though the man is reading a printed text. No emotion comes through. Takahashi, of course, has absolutely no idea what he is talking about.

"Hey, wait a minute," Takahashi says, his voice louder than before. But his words seem not to reach the man at the other end, who goes on talking in those same unaccented tones as though leaving a message on voice mail.

"We're going to tap you on the shoulder someday. We know what you look like."

"What the hell . . ."

"If somebody taps you on the shoulder somewhere someday, it's us," the man says.

Takahashi has no idea what he should say in response to this. He keeps silent. Having been left in a refrigerator case for a while, the phone feels uncomfortably cold in his hand.

"You might forget what you did, but we will never forget."

"Hey, I don't know what's going on here, but I'm telling you you've got the wrong guy," Takahashi says.

"You'll never get away."

The connection is cut. The circuit goes dead. The final message lies abandoned on a deserted beach. Takahashi stares at the cell phone in his hand. He has no idea who the man's "we" are or who was meant to receive the call, but the sound of the voice remains in his ear—the one with the deformed earlobe—like an absurd curse that leaves a bad aftertaste. He has a smooth, cold feeling in his hand, as if he has just grabbed a snake.

Somebody, for some reason, is being chased by a number of people, Takahashi imagines. Judging from the man's declarative tone, that somebody will probably never get away. Sometime, somewhere, when he is least expecting it, someone is going to tap him on the shoulder. What will happen after that?

In any case, it has nothing to do with me, Takahashi tells himself. This is one of many violent, bloody acts being performed in secret on the hidden side of the city—things from another world that come in on another circuit. *I'm just an innocent passerby. All I did was pick up a cell phone ringing on a convenience-store shelf out of kindness. I figured somebody called because he was trying to track down his lost cell phone.*

He closes the phone and puts it back where he found it, next to a box of Camembert cheese wedges. *Better not have anything to do with this cell phone anymore. Better get out of here as fast as I can. Better get as far away from that dangerous circuit as I can.* He hurries over to the register, grabs a fistful of change from his pocket, and pays for his sandwich and milk.

a.m.

*T*akahashi alone on a park bench. The little park with the cats. No one else around. Two swings side by side, withered leaves covering the ground. Moon up in the sky. He takes his own cell phone from his coat pocket and punches in a number.

The Alphaville room where Mari is. The phone rings. She wakes at the fourth or fifth ring and looks at her watch with a frown. She stands up and takes the receiver.

"Hello," Mari says, her voice uncertain.

"Hi, it's me. Were you sleeping?"

"A little," Mari says. She covers the mouthpiece and clears her throat. "It's okay. I was just napping in a chair."

"Wanna go for breakfast? At that restaurant I told you about with the great omelets? I'm pretty sure they have other good stuff, too."

"Practice over?" Mari asks, but she hardly recognizes her own voice. *I am me and not me.*

"It sure is. And I'm starved. How about you?"

"Not really, tell you the truth. I feel more like going home."

"That's okay, too. I'll walk you to the station. I think the trains have started running."

"I'm sure I can walk from here to the station by myself," Mari says.

"I'd like to talk to you some more if possible. Let's talk on the way to the station. If you don't mind."

"No, I don't mind."

"I'll be there in ten minutes. Okay?"

"Okay," Mari says.

Takahashi cuts the connection, folds his phone, and puts it in his pocket. He gets up from the park bench, takes one big stretch, and looks up at the sky. Still dark. The same crescent moon is floating there. Strange that, viewed from one spot in the predawn city, such a big solid object could be hanging there free of charge.

"You'll never get away," Takahashi says aloud while looking at the crescent moon.

The enigmatic ring of those words will remain inside Takahashi as a kind of metaphor. "You'll never get away. . . . You might forget what you did, but we will never forget," the man on the phone said. The more Takahashi thinks about their meaning, the more it seems to him that the words were intended not for someone else but for him—directly, personally. Maybe it was no accident. Maybe the cell phone was lurking on that convenience-store shelf, waiting specifically for him to pass by. "We," Takahashi thinks. *Who could this "we" possibly be? And what will "we" never forget?*

Takahashi slings his instrument case and his tote bag over his shoulder and starts walking toward the Alphaville at a leisurely pace. As he walks, he rubs the whiskers that have begun to sprout on his cheeks. The final darkness of the night envelops the city like a thin skin. Garbage trucks begin to appear on the streets. As they collect their loads and move on, people who have spent the night in various parts of the city begin to take their place, walking toward subway stations, intent upon catching those first trains that will take them out to the suburbs, like schools of fish swimming upstream. People who have finally finished the work they must do all night, young people who are tired from playing all night: whatever the differences in their situations, both types are equally reticent. Even the young couple who stop at a drink vending machine, tightly pressed against each other, have no more words for each other. Instead, what they soundlessly share is the lingering warmth of their bodies.

The new day is almost here, but the old one is still dragging its heavy skirts. Just as ocean water and river water struggle against each other at a river mouth, the old time and the new time clash and blend. Takahashi is unable to tell for sure which side—which world—contains his center of gravity.

17

Mari and Takahashi are walking down the street side by side. Mari has her bag slung over her shoulder and her Red Sox hat pulled low over her eyes. She is not wearing her glasses.

"You're not tired?" Takahashi asks.

Mari shakes her head. "I had a little nap."

"Once after an all-night practice like this, I got on the Chuo Line at Shinjuku to go home, and I woke up way out in the country in Yamanashi. Mountains all around. Not to boast, but I'm the type who can fall fast asleep just about anywhere."

Mari remains silent, as if she is thinking about something else.

"Anyhow, to get back to what we were talking about before . . . about Eri Asai," Takahashi says. "Of course, you don't have to talk about her if you don't want to. But just let me ask you something."

"Okay."

"Your sister has been sleeping for a long time. And she has no intention of waking up. You said something like that, right?"

"Right."

"I don't know what's going on, but could she be in a coma or some kind of unconscious state?"

Mari falters briefly. "No, that's not it," she says. "I don't think it's anything life-threatening at the moment. She's . . . just asleep."

"Just asleep?" Takahashi asks.

"Uh-huh, except . . ." Mari sighs. "Sorry, but I don't think I'm ready to talk about it."

"That's okay. If you're not ready, don't talk."

"I'm tired, and I can't get my head straight. And my voice doesn't sound like my voice to me."

"That's okay. Some other time. Let's drop it for now."

"Okay," Mari says with obvious relief.

For some moments, they don't talk about anything at all. They simply walk toward the station. Takahashi quietly whistles a tune.

"I wonder what time it starts to get light out," Mari says.

Takahashi looks at his watch. "At this season . . . hmm . . . maybe six forty. This is when the nights are longest. It'll stay dark a while."

"When it's dark, it really makes you tired, doesn't it?"

"That's when everybody's supposed to be asleep," Takahashi says. "Historically speaking, it's quite a recent development that human beings have felt easy about going out after dark. It used to be after the sun set, people would just crawl into their caves and protect themselves. Our internal clocks are still set for us to sleep after the sun goes down."

"It feels like a *really long* time since it got dark last night."

"Well, it *has* been a long time."

They walk past a drugstore with a large truck parked out front. The driver is unloading the truck's contents through the store's half-open shutter.

"Think I can see you again sometime soon?" Takahashi asks.

"Why?"

"Why? 'Cause I want to see you and talk to you some more. At a more normal time of day if possible."

"You mean, like, a date?"

"Maybe you could call it that."

"What could you talk about with me?"

Takahashi thinks about this. "Are you asking me what kind of subject matter we have in common?"

"Aside from Eri, that is."

"Hmm . . . common subject matter . . . put it to me like that all of a sudden, and I can't think of anything concrete. Right this second. It just seems to me we'd have plenty to talk about if we got together."

"Talking to me wouldn't be much fun."

"Did anybody ever say that to you—like, you're not much fun to talk to?"

Mari shakes her head. "No, not really."

"So you've got nothing to worry about."

"I *have* been told I've got a darkish personality. A few times."

Takahashi swings his trombone case from his right shoulder to his left. Then he says, "It's not as if our lives are divided simply into light and dark. There's a shadowy middle ground. Recognizing and understanding the shadows is what a healthy intelligence does. And to acquire a healthy intelligence takes a certain amount of time and effort. I don't think you have a particularly dark character."

Mari thinks about Takahashi's words. "I *am* a coward, though," she says.

"Now there you're wrong. A cowardly girl doesn't go out alone like this in the city at night. You wanted to discover something here. Right?"

"What do you mean, 'here'?"

"Someplace different: someplace outside your usual territory."

"I wonder if I discovered something—here."

Takahashi smiles and looks at Mari. "Anyhow, I want to see you and talk to you again at least one more time. That's what I'd like to do."

Mari looks at Takahashi. Their eyes meet.

"That might be impossible," she says.

"Impossible?"

"Uh-huh."

"You mean you and I might never meet again?"

"Realistically speaking," Mari says.

"Are you seeing somebody?"

"Not really, now."

"So you just don't like me?"

Mari shakes her head. "I'm not saying that. I won't be in Japan after next Monday. I'm leaving for Beijing. To be a kind of exchange student there until next June at least."

"Of *course*," Takahashi says, impressed. "You're such an outstanding student."

"I applied on the off chance they'd pick me—and they did. I'm just a freshman, I figured there was no way I could get in, but I guess it's a kind of special program."

"That's great! Congratulations."

"So, anyhow, I've just got a few days till I leave, and I'll probably be so busy getting ready . . ."

"Of course."

"Of course what?"

"You've got to get ready to leave for Beijing, you'll be busy with all kinds of stuff, and you won't have time to see me. Of course," Takahashi says. "I understand perfectly. That's okay, I don't mind. I can wait."

"But I won't be coming back to Japan for six months or more."

"I may not look it, but I can be a very patient guy. And killing time is one of my specialties. Give me your address over there, okay? I want to write to you."

"I don't mind, I guess."

"If I write, will you answer me?"

"Uh-huh," Mari says.

"And when you come back to Japan next summer, let's have that date or whatever you want to call it. We can go to the zoo or the botanical garden or the aquarium, and then we'll have the most politically correct and scrumptious omelets we can find."

Mari looks at Takahashi again—straight in the eyes, as if to verify something.

"But why should you be interested in me?"

"Good question. I can't explain it myself right this second. But maybe—just maybe—if we start getting together and talking, after a while something like Francis

Lai's soundtrack music will start playing in the background, and a whole slew of concrete reasons why I'm
interested in you will line up out of nowhere. With luck, it
might even snow for us."

When they reach the station, Mari takes a small red
notebook from her pocket, writes down her Beijing
address, tears the page out, and hands it to Takahashi.
Takahashi folds it in two and slips it into his billfold.

"Thanks," he says. "I'll write you a nice long letter."

Mari comes to a halt before the automatic ticket gate,
thinking about something. She is unsure whether she
should tell him what is on her mind.

"I remembered something about Eri before," she says,
once she has decided to go ahead. "I had forgotten about
it for a long time, but it came back to me all of a sudden
after you called me at the hotel and I was spacing out in
the chair. I wonder if I should just tell you about it here
and now."

"Of course you should."

"I'd like to tell somebody about it while the memory is
fresh," Mari says. "Otherwise, the details might disappear."

Takahashi touches his ear to signal his readiness to
listen.

"When I was in kindergarten," Mari begins, "Eri and
I once got trapped in the elevator of our building. I
think there must have been an earthquake. The elevator
made this tremendous shake between floors and stopped
dead. The lights went out, and we were in total darkness.
I mean *total*: you couldn't see your own hand. There was
nobody else on the elevator, just the two of us. Well, I
panicked: I completely stiffened up. It was like I turned

into a fossil right then and there. I couldn't move a finger.
I could hardly breathe, couldn't make a sound. Eri called
my name, but I couldn't answer. I just fogged over: it was
like my brain went numb and Eri's voice was barely reach-
ing me through a crack."

Mari closes her eyes for a moment and relives the darkness in her mind.

She goes on with her story. "I don't remember how long
the darkness lasted. Now it seems awfully long to me, but
in fact it may not have been that long. Exactly how many
minutes it lasted—five minutes, twenty minutes—really
doesn't matter. The important thing is that during that
whole time in the dark, Eri was holding me. And it wasn't
just some ordinary hug. She squeezed me so hard our two
bodies felt as if they were melting into one. She never
loosened her grip for a second. It felt as though if we
separated the slightest bit, we would never see each other
in this world again."

Takahashi leans against the ticket gate, saying nothing, as he waits for the rest of Mari's story. Mari pulls
her right hand from the pocket of her varsity jacket
and stares at it for a while. Then, raising her face, she
goes on:

"Of course, Eri was scared to death, too, I'm sure.
Maybe even as scared as I was. She must have wanted to
scream and cry. I mean, she was just a second-grader,
after all. But she stayed calm. She probably decided on
the spot that she was going to be strong. She made up her
mind that she would have to be the strong big sister for
my sake. And the whole time she kept whispering in my
ear stuff like, 'We're gonna be okay. There's nothing to be

afraid of. I'm here with you, and somebody's gonna come and help soon.' She sounded totally calm. Like a grown-up. She even sang me songs, though I don't remember what they were. I wanted to sing with her, but I couldn't. I was so scared my voice wouldn't come out. But Eri just kept singing for me all by herself. I entrusted myself completely to her arms. The two of us became one: there were no gaps between us. We even shared a single heart-beat. Then suddenly the lights came on, and the elevator shook again and started to move."

Mari inserts a pause. She is backtracking through her memory, looking for the words.

"But that was the last time. That was . . . how should I say it? . . . the one moment in my life when I was able to draw closest to Eri . . . the one moment when she and I joined heart to heart as one: there was nothing separating us. After that, it seems, we grew farther and farther apart. We separated, and before long we were living in different worlds. That sense of union I felt in the darkness of the elevator, that strong bond between our hearts, never came back again. I don't know what went wrong, but we were never able to go back to where we started from."

Takahashi reaches out and takes Mari's hand. She is momentarily startled but doesn't pull her hand from his. Takahashi keeps his gentle grip on her hand—her small, soft hand—for a very long time.

"I don't really want to go," Mari says.

"To China?"

"Uh-huh."

"Why not?"

"'Cause I'm scared."

"That's only natural," he says. "You're going to a strange, far-off place all by yourself."

"I know."

"You'll be fine, though," he says. "I know you. And I'll be waiting for you here."

Mari nods.

"You're very pretty," he says. "Did you know that?"

Mari looks up at Takahashi. Then she withdraws her hand from his and puts it into the pocket of her varsity jacket. Her eyes drop to her feet. She is checking to make sure her yellow sneakers are still clean.

"Thanks. But I want to go home now."

"I'll write to you," he says. "A super-long letter, like in an old-fashioned novel."

"Okay," Mari says.

She goes in through the ticket gate, walks to the platform, and disappears into a waiting express train. Takahashi watches her go. Soon the departure signal sounds, the doors close, and the train pulls away from the platform. When he loses sight of the train, Takahashi picks his instrument case up from the floor, slings the strap over his shoulder, and heads for his own station, whistling softly. The number of people moving through this station gradually increases.

 a.m.

18

Eri Asai's room.

Outside the window, the day is growing brighter. Eri Asai is asleep in her bed. Her expression and pose are the same as when we last saw her. A thick cloak of sleep envelops her.

Mari enters the room. She opens the door quietly to avoid being noticed by the other members of the family, steps in, and closes the door just as quietly. The silence and chill of the room make her somewhat tense. She stands in front of the door, examining the contents of her sister's room with great care. First she checks to be sure that this is indeed the room as she has always known it—that nothing has been disturbed, that nothing or no one unfamiliar is lurking in a corner. Then she approaches the bed and looks down at her soundly sleeping sister. She reaches out and gently touches Eri's forehead, quietly calling her name. There is absolutely no response. As always. Mari drags over the swivel chair from its place by the desk and sits down. She leans forward and observes her sister's face close-up as if searching for the meaning of a sign hidden there.

Some five minutes go by. Mari stands up, takes off her Red Sox cap, and smooths out her crumpled hair. Then she removes her wristwatch and lays it on her sister's desk. She takes off her varsity jacket, her hooded sweatshirt, and the striped flannel shirt under that, leaving only a white T-shirt. She takes off her thick sport socks and blue jeans, and then she burrows softly into her sister's bed. She lets her body adapt to being under the covers, after which she lays a thin arm across the body of her sister, who is sleeping face-up. She gently presses her cheek against her sister's chest and holds herself there, listening, hoping to understand each beat of her sister's heart. Her eyes are gently closed as she listens. Soon, without warning, tears begin to ooze from her closed eyes—large tears, and totally natural. They course down her cheek and moisten the pajamas of her sleeping sister.

Mari sits up in bed and wipes the tears from her cheeks with her fingertips. Toward something—exactly what, she has no concrete idea—she feels that she has committed some utterly inexcusable act, something she can never undo. The emotion has struck with great suddenness, and with no tangible connection to what has come before, but it is overwhelming. The tears continue to pour out of her. She catches them in the palms of her hands. Each new falling tear is warm, like blood, with the heat from inside her body. Suddenly it occurs to Mari: *I could have been in some other place than this. And Eri, too: she could have been in some other place than this.*

To reassure herself, Mari takes one more look around the room, and then again she looks down at her sister. Eri is beautiful in her sleep—truly beautiful. Mari almost wishes she could preserve that face of hers in a glass case. Consciousness just happens to be missing from it at the moment: it may have gone into hiding, but it must certainly be flowing somewhere out of sight, far below the surface, like a vein of water. Mari can hear its faint reverberations. She listens for them. *The place where they originate is not that far from here. And Eri's flow is almost certainly blending with my own,* Mari feels. *We are sisters, after all.*

Mari bends over and briefly presses her lips to Eri's. She raises her head and looks down at her sister's face again. She allows time to pass through her heart. Again she kisses Eri: a longer, softer kiss. Mari feels almost as if she is kissing herself. Mari and Eri: one syllable's difference. She smiles. Then, as if relieved, she curls up to sleep beside her big sister—to bond with her if possible, to share the warmth of their two bodies, to exchange signs of life with her.

"Come back, Eri," she whispers in her sister's ear. "*Please* come back." She closes her eyes and allows the strength to leave her body. With her eyes closed, sleep comes for her, enveloping her like a great, soft wave from the open sea. Her tears have stopped.

The brightness outside the window is increasing with great speed. Vivid streaks of light stream into the room through gaps in the shade. The old temporality is losing its effectiveness and moving into the background. Many people go on mumbling the old words, but in the light of the newly revealed sun, the meanings of words are shifting rapidly and are being renewed. Even supposing that most of the new meanings are temporary things that will persist only through sundown that day, we will be spending time and moving forward with them.

In the corner of the room, the TV screen seems to flash momentarily. Light might be rising to the surface of the picture tube. Something might be starting to move there, perhaps the trembling of an image. Could the circuit be trying to reconnect? We hold our breath and watch its progress. In the next second, however, the screen is showing nothing. The only thing there is blankness.

Perhaps what we *thought* we saw was just an optical illusion, a mere reflection of a momentary fluctuation in the light streaming through the window. The room is still dominated by silence, but its depth and weight have clearly diminished and retreated. Now the cries of birds reach our ears. If we could further sharpen our auditory sense, we might be able to hear bicycles on the street or people talking to each other or the weather report on the radio. We might even be able to hear bread toasting. The lavish morning light washes every corner of the world at no charge. Two young sisters sleep peacefully, their bodies pressed together in one small bed. We are probably the only ones who know that.

*I*nside the 7-Eleven. Checklist in hand, the clerk is kneeling in an aisle, taking an inventory. Japanese hip-hop is playing. This is the same young man who received Takahashi's payment at the cash register. Skinny, hair dyed rusty red. Tired at the end of his night shift, he yawns frequently. He hears, intermingled with the music, the ringing of a cell phone. He stands up and looks around. Then he checks each of the aisles. There are no customers. He is the only one in the store, but the cell phone keeps ringing stubbornly. Very strange. He searches all parts of the store and finally discovers the phone on a shelf in the dairy case.

Who in the hell forgets a cell phone in a place like this? Must be some crazy dude. With a cluck of the tongue and a look of disgust, he picks up the chilled device, presses the talk button, and holds the receiver to his ear.

"Hello," he says.

"You probably think you got away with it," announces a male voice devoid of intonation.

"Hello?!" the clerk shouts.

"But you can't get away. You can run, but you'll never

be able to get away." A short, suggestive silence follows, and then the connection is cut.

a.m.

Allowing ourselves to become pure point of view, we hang in midair over the city. What we see now is a gigantic metropolis waking up. Commuter trains of many colors move in all directions, transporting people from place to place. Each of those under transport is a human being with a different face and mind, and at the same time each is a nameless part of the collective entity. Each is simultaneously a self-contained whole and a mere part. Handling this dualism of theirs skillfully and advantageously, they perform their morning rituals with deftness and precision: brushing teeth, shaving, tying neckties, applying lipstick. They check the morning news on TV, exchange words with their families, eat, and defecate.

With daybreak the crows flock in, scavenging for food. Their oily black wings shine in the morning sun. Dualism is not as important an issue for the crows as for the human beings. Their single most important concern is securing sufficient nourishment for individual maintenance. The garbage trucks have not yet collected all of the garbage. This is a gigantic city, after all, and it produces a prodigious volume of garbage. Raising raucous cries, the crows soar down to all parts of the city like dive bombers.

The new sun pours new light on the city streets. The glass of high-rise buildings sparkles blindingly. There is not a speck of cloud to be seen in the sky, just a haze of smog hanging along the horizon. The crescent moon takes the form of a silent white monolith, a long-lost message floating in the western sky. A news helicopter dances through the sky like a nervous insect, sending images of traffic conditions back to the station. Cars trying to enter the city have already started lining up at the tollbooths of the Metropolitan Expressway. Chilly shadows still lie over many streets sandwiched between tall buildings. Most of last night's memories remain there untouched.

a.m.

Our point of view departs from the sky over city center and shifts to an area above a quiet suburban residential neighborhood. Below us stand rows of two-story houses with yards. From above, all the houses look much alike—similar incomes, similar family makeup. A new dark blue Volvo proudly reflects the morning sun. A golf practice net set up on one lawn. Morning papers freshly delivered. People walking large dogs. The sounds of meal preparations from kitchen windows. People calling out to each other. Here, too, a brand-new day is beginning. It could be a day like all the others, or it could be a day remarkable enough in many ways to remain in the memory. In either case, for now, for most people, it is a blank sheet of paper.

We choose one house from among all the similar houses and drop straight down to it. Passing through the glass and the lowered cream-colored shade of a second-story window, we soundlessly enter Eri Asai's room.

Mari is sleeping in the bed, cuddled against her sister. We can hear her quiet breathing. As far as we can see, her sleep is peaceful. She seems to have warmed up: her cheeks have more color than before. Her bangs cover her eyes. Could she be dreaming? Or is the hint of a smile on her lips the trace of a memory? Mari has made her way through the long hours of darkness, traded many words with the night people she encountered there, and come back to where she belongs. For now, at least, there is nothing nearby to threaten her. Nineteen years old, she is protected by a roof and walls, protected, too, by fenced green lawns, burglar alarms, newly waxed station wagons, and big, smart dogs that stroll the neighborhood. The morning sun shining in the window gently envelops and warms her. Mari's left hand rests on the black hair of her sister spread upon the pillow, her fingers softly opened in a natural curve.

And as for Eri, we can see no change in either her pose or her expression. She seems totally unaware that her little sister has crawled into bed and is sleeping beside her.

Eventually, Eri's small mouth does move slightly, as if

in response to something. A quick trembling of the lips that lasts but an instant, perhaps a tenth of a second. Finely honed pure point of view that we are, however, we cannot overlook this movement. Our eyes take positive note of this momentary physical signal. The trembling might well be a minuscule quickening of something to come. Or it might be the barest hint of a minuscule quickening. Whatever it is, something is trying to send a sign to this side through a tiny opening in the consciousness. Such an impression comes to us with certainty.

Unimpeded by other schemes, this hint of things to come takes time to expand in the new morning light, and we attempt to watch it unobtrusively, with deep concentration. The night has begun to open up at last. There will be time until the next darkness arrives.

A NOTE ON THE TYPE

This book was set in Caledonia, a typeface designed by
W. A. Dwiggins (1880–1956). It belongs to the family of printing
types called "modern face" by printers—a term used to mark the
change in style of the type letters that occurred around 1800.
Caledonia borders on the general design of Scotch Roman
but it is more freely drawn than that letter. This version of
Caledonia was adapted by David Berlow in 1979.

COMPOSED BY

Creative Graphics, Allentown, Pennsylvania

PRINTED AND BOUND BY

Berryville Graphics, Berryville, Virginia

DESIGNED BY

Iris Weinstein